RAGWARS

RAGWARS

by Alice Bach

A YEARLING BOOK

Published by
Dell Publishing Co., Inc.
1 Dag Hammarskjold Plaza
New York, New York 10017

Yearling ® TM 913705, Dell Publishing Co., Inc.

ISBN: 0-440-47345-4

Printed in the United States of America

October 1987

10 9 8 7 6 5 4 3 2 1

CW

For Jay Smith
and
José Vidal

Chapter One

"There will be a special assembly in the auditorium at eleven o'clock this morning. Each class period will be shortened by fifteen minutes to accommodate this emergency meeting."

"Oh, rats! A lecture on the dangers of talking to strange men seen around the building," Stanwyck groaned.

"It could be something cheery," I reminded my friends. "Like an award given to the school for overall excellence. Or we all got into the colleges of our choice."

Nobody was buying that one.

"Maybe it's about not going to the video games parlor where that kid was mugged a few months ago."

"Clever, Meg. An emergency meeting three months after the fact? Besides, no one hangs out at that grody place," insisted Stanwyck. "It's got to be a strange man."

Lulie Billingsley was sketching in her history notebook. Each page of her notes was perfect, like a Valentine, written in swirly script. She corralled all her doodling to a separate page that she could rip out. Maybe she's willed her notebooks to some museum. The perfect high school student.

We were all wrong about the emergency. Our principal, Mr. Percy Dalton-Worthington, strode onto the stage and raised his hand for silence. "We have a great deal to cover today, girls, so we will dispense with the formalities. At the request of the, ah, Federal Bureau—ah"—he licked his lips— "one of the government agencies, we have been asked to acquaint our students with a burgeoning problem among teen-agers."

Whispers could be heard all over the auditorium: "Birth control, dope, wine, abortion."

"A situation I am certain we do not have here at the Benchley School for Girls," he continued.

Stanwyck slid down in her seat. "So what's the problem, old boy? Teddy-bear flu?"

"To explain the situation and the law, we have with us this morning Mr. Maxwell Weissenstat, area director of the FBI." A gasp went through the students and faculty. Stanwyck sat up straight. "Now this is worth the price of admission."

Lulie punched Stan's knee. "Shut up. What could the FBI want with us? They must have the wrong school."

Mr. FBI looked like a weasel. Central Casting couldn't have sent us a better model of a highly nervous operative in a too-sharp three-piece suit. All he needed was a shoe with a built-in microphone to complete the picture of a sitcom agent. We all relaxed. No situation that this man was in charge of could be life-threatening or even mildly serious.

"Good morning, girls. I am delighted that Mr. Worthy-Dalton has given me the opportunity to talk with you today. As most of you know, computers are wonderful machines. In the right hands, used responsibly, they are little extra brains for all of us."

"I'm going to throw up," Stan growled. "He thinks we're in kindergarten."

"We at the Bureau use computers every day."

Nora's eyes grew wide. "He thinks we're retarded."

"And we use computers within the law." He leaned forward on the podium, gripping his pointer. "Do you know that using a computer to invade someone else's databank without permission is a crime? If you use pirated access codes to look around in some corporate databank, you are as guilty of a crime as if you took a crowbar and jimmied the door of the company some dark night to steal their files."

"We can thank you and your fancy footwork for this meeting, Baum," Lulie snapped.

"Get serious," Stan snapped back. "I wasn't the one keyboarding with crooks. Isn't that right, Nora?"

Nora appealed to me. "You promised she'd never mention Tim's little mistake again."

A few months earlier Stan and I had solved a series of robberies that Tim Mooney had masterminded. Unfortunately, Stan had become too sure of herself. We had done some fancy footwork ourselves, invading the police computers, trying to hook up the common denominator in each of the robberies. Now was not the time to remind Stan of this.

"You girls probably think I'm a stodgy old federal cop. Well, I guess I am." The FBI agent grinned broadly to show he didn't believe a word of it. "Law enforcement is a serious business. We're responsible to the President and to the people of this country for protecting their rights of privacy against the hackers who prowl around databanks."

"FBI six, kids nothing." Stanwyck muttered.

"To prove to you that we're not fooling around with teen hackers any longer, we have with us today a former hacker, a fellow who will tell you firsthand what it's like to run afoul of the FBI."

A dazzling tall blond guy in a tweed jacket and jeans ambled onto the stage. His hair fell forward across his face. As he spoke, he tossed his hair out of his eyes, giving himself a devilish air. He wasn't the feds' best choice for scaring kids away from hacking. I'd learn how to hack just to be near him!

"I am Freddy Frobisher," he began. "I've been hacking since I was twelve. My first computer was a nothing Commodore—"

"True confessions. And it's all wasted on us," Lulie murmured. "I wouldn't know a Commodore from a king. Why don't they just scare Baum and let the rest of us go back to class?"

"Think of it this way, Lulie. If they held the heavy-duty meetings in this school only for the smart kids, you'd never get told about anything, except the parties."

". . . my father had one of the original Altair micros. We were running some simple machine-language programs off the Altair and an Apple 1. I was writing code before I could write script."

There was an undercurrent buzz in the auditorium. Mr. FBI crossed the stage and whispered something to his stooge. Unruffled, Freddy tossed back his glorious hair and began again. "What I'm here to tell you is simple. The government is getting tough with hackers. If you're keyboarding without regard to the law, be warned. The FBI may appear at your door, confiscate your computer equipment, and put you on trial as an adult for computer crime. Be careful when you're cruising the bulletin boards. Many of the so-called pirate boards are being scrutinized by the feds. That guy with a cute handle may well be an undercover agent. They are on to all the tricks. So play it smart."

We all shifted around in our seats. It was hard to panic about threats of computer crime and getting entangled with the FBI. Probably no more than ten people owned a computer in the entire school.

Mr. Dalton-Worthington lumbered onto the stage. "Any questions?"

Stan's hand shot into the air. "What's the responsibility of the sysop? I mean, how can you regulate who uses your board?"

"That is a gray area at the moment," answered the agent.

"Good going, Stanwyck." I squeezed her arm.

"What's a sysop?" asked Lulie.

"A person who runs a bulletin board. Stands for systems operator. Like myself." She raised her hand again. "I run a board, Freddy, called the Headboard. Mostly locals, for messages and chat about games. We have Zork and Enchanter groups—nothing spectacular. But I've read about sysops having their entire systems closed down when people have dropped illegal access codes onto their boards apparently without their knowledge."

"Better tighten up who has access to your message facilities," advised Freddy. "I'd scan the messages for odd codes every couple of days. And delete any messages that look crufty. Just erase 'em. Any hacker will understand why you're doing it."

"The important thing, girls," the principal said, "is to remember that even if the law isn't clear about all the fine points of hacking, we all know it is wrong. And educated people choose to live moral lives." Our principal smiled, his long yellow horse teeth bared.

"Untrue to the max," Nora chirped beside me. "We read in social studies that white-collar crime is the fastest-growing criminal element in our society."

Oblivious to Nora's voice of dissent, Mr. Dalton-Worthington rumbled on. "If there are no more questions, we will stand and sing the first and last verse of 'God Bless America.' "

Stanwyck grabbed my hand and edged out of our row while everyone else was singing about the land of the free and the home of the brave. "I want to talk to Freddy," she said, dragging me up the aisle, "up close and personal."

"You're crazy. We've got to get to class."

"I can pick up a lot of tips from that guy. He probably knows more than Martin."

Martin is Stanwyck's hacking buddy, known by the handle Captain Midnight. A short, dark kid with ink stains on his hands, he would lose to Freddy in every category I could name.

"I thought you had more loyalty than that," I said as we approached Miss Sammon, who was guarding the door.

"We have to go to the girls' room." Stanwyck smiled sweetly.

"One at a time."

"Nature has called *both* of us," Stan whispered, theatrically clutching her stomach.

12

"I want both of you girls in your next class in five minutes. Is that clear?"

I trailed my hand over my forehead. "It must have been the pot roast."

We circled around the auditorium and waited at the end of the corridor near the principal's office. As soon as the singing stopped, Mr. Dalton-Worthington hurried out the door with his hand on the FBI agent's arm. Our luck was holding. Freddy was not with them.

Standing in front of the full-length mirror combing his hair was the Hacker Prince. "So they caught you," Stan said, striding up to him. "Nasty break."

"Impounded all my equipment and held it for six months. Made this deal where they trot me out at schools to scare other kids with tales of my wickedness. This is the first girls' school. Must have been a glitch in the program. I bet you lovelies don't know a disk drive from a lipstick. By the way, do you know the name of that tall, gorgeous girl wearing a dark green sweater and skirt? She was sitting near you two in the assembly."

"I think you mean the new girl. I can't remember her name. She just started last week. She's from England, I think." I had to admire his eye. All the way from the stage, he had picked the best-looking girl out of the sea of faces in the audience.

"I run 640K on my PC," Stanwyck said crisply. "I have an 8087 math coprocessor, 10mg hard disk and networking capability through orchidnet."

Freddy jerked around as though he'd been shot. He turned to me. "I suppose you write machine code and crunch numbers to pass the time."

"I'm Jess Graham." I smiled through slitted eyes. "We have a couple of questions to ask you if you can spare a moment."

"I sure can," he said. Then he added, "Listen, I didn't mean to come on like some macho pig. Girls who write their own code? I've died and gone to heaven."

I looked away from his eager smile. I did know the difference between a disk drive and a lipstick. But that about corked my computer hardware expertise. Stan had taught me to use word-processing software and how to answer the messages on Headboard, but I had no idea how any of it worked. There could be four miniature wizards living inside the machine working very fast and very quietly, for all I knew.

"I can give you the names of some swift sysops, but we have to be cool. You know a board called Funhouse?" he asked.

Stan shook her head.

"It's an elite Apple board run by a friend of mine in Chicago. He's a real wire-head. Mostly cracking—what a bandit!"

"Cracking?" I hoped I didn't sound too bush.

"You know, pirating, breaking the back of the software codes, swapping."

Stan edged closer to Freddy, forcing me to drop back a few steps. "Sure I know. I cruise Nibbles Away sometimes. I follow their postings. But they only crack Apple programs."

"They are the easiest to get into," Freddy said. "Apple is a good hacking computer. Codes are plain. I probably have six or seven hundred games for the Apple."

"Could you give me some good board numbers?" Stan

14

asked. "Now that I'm sysoping, I want to talk to other sysops, maybe swap cracking files so I can have a really current board."

"Got to be cool. They think cracking's a crime, although you can copy tapes and records without some agent hammering on your door and copping your recording equipment. It's totally unfair. Give me your notebook, Stanwyck. Jess, watch the door. That retrograde agent moves as quick as a snake."

For several minutes Stan and Freddy squatted on the stage swapping information about online programs and bulletin-board numbers. He gave her the names of several sysops in the New York area, and they arranged to get together online as soon as he got back to Minneapolis.

"This teach-'em-a-lesson program has turned out to be a cloud with a silver lining. I meet a lot of hackers in each school and pass on access codes, all under the watchful eye of the FBI."

"What a trip!" Stan's face was filled with admiration.

"You might give the girl in green my phone number," he said with a sly smile. I couldn't decide if he was teasing or not.

The second bell rang, and we fled to class.

"Good-bye, Jess. Try Risky Business, it's a hot board."

"His regular handle is Magnetic Surger," whispered Stan as we slipped into French class several minutes late. Magnetic, I thought, writing *Freddy Frobisher* in the margin of my French grammer book. Definitely magnetic.

We were sitting in Stanwyck's room working on Headboard. About once a week we have to do housekeeping chores on the board. That means running through all the

15

notices that have been posted, deleting the scummy ones, pulling out the names and addresses of new callers, answering any pertinent questions on the board. It's a great deal of work maintaining a bulletin board, but Stanwyck has been devoted to it for three months. Of course, there is a fun part of the Board. And that's chatting with callers, getting a network of friends all over the country. She has a list of regulars about as long as my arm.

"Jess, will you update the news section? I'm erasing the article about the kid who swallows golf balls. We've had it running almost a month."

This is my steady assignment. We have a mininewspaper with hilarious news that turns up in real newspapers. Every couple weeks we pull out the stale articles and key in new ones. I try to find weird and unusual facts about people and animals. Last week there was an article about a gorilla who had lived in a city zoo for twenty-five years. He was about forty, the oldest gorilla in captivity. It seems the zoo folk gave him a special birthday party, and the gorilla stuffed himself with gorilla birthday cake and died a few hours later.

As we worked, the screen lit up and the system beeped now and then as people called the board. Stan dreams of the time when her board will be busy twenty hours a day. She averages about ten calls a day now, which we've been told is good for such a new board. If we were a pirate board or a phreaker board we'd be busier, but we'd also be illegal and shivering every time there was a knock at the door.

Most of our callers are regulars. There is one guy—Mr. Rogers is his handle—who calls the board every night at seven and asks to speak to the sysop. The system beeps, alerting Stanwyck that one of the callers wants to chat. She

16

activates the computer and types answers to his questions for as long as an hour. It's been going on about a month. He won't give her his real name, and he won't talk "voice," meaning on the regular telephone. He'll just type messages from his computer screen to hers through the anonymous safety of the bulletin board.

Mr. Rogers's big interest is fantasy games. Stan has one section of her board devoted to tips and hints about fantasy games like Zork and Ultima. Mr. Rogers offers hints to other players every day. He's into all the games and seems to have played them to the max.

Stanwyck scrolled through the new postings, pulling out the scrofulous ones. Some people abuse the boards, leaving foul messages merely to bug the sysop. Electronic bathroom grafitti. "Look, Jess, there's someone recommending Risky Business. Isn't that the board Freddy Frobisher mentioned?"

We immediately dialed the number and posted a message on the board suggesting the sysop call Archangel of the Headboard. His board advertised more than three hundred cracked programs. It's the new hot computer gig, now that phreakers are going underground. Kids swap software programs like baseball cards, often not even running the ware once they've downloaded it. It's more of a greed-and-brag thing, how many programs do you have, rather than how many have you used.

We switched the Headboard back on, and within minutes the system beeped. It was Mr. Rogers, calling to ask Stan if she wanted to run a new solve-and-hint sheet for a fantasy game he was playing called Questra. I wondered why he didn't have a fantasy handle like Enchanter or Sorcerer or Vogon. Some of the handles on Stanwyck's board are bizarre:

17

Seastalker, Infidel, Cutthroat (all of them are from games, I think). Some are more unusual—King of the Road, Zapper, Dynamicro, Micro-Mogul, and all matter of computer puns.

Stanwyck was typing away frantically, muttering under her breath as if she were having a genuine conversation with Mr. Rogers. "I can't keep up with all the fantasy games. There are hundreds. But I do want to keep the Hitchhiker hints current. That seems to be the most popular."

Tell Numero Uno who is stuck on Hitchhiker: Try lying down in front of the bulldozer. I'm tired of leaving him notes. He never thanks me. And he never swaps for any hints I need.

Stanwyck signed off. "Poor old Mr. Rogers is very grumpy today. Somebody probably hid his sweater."

"Wonder why he uses such a babyish handle?" I said.

"It's weird. Haven't seen that handle posted on any other boards. Maybe he has a variety of handles. He's so secretive, he probably doesn't want to be traced."

I wasn't convinced. "But he calls you every day. And he posts notes all over your board. He gets angry if kids don't respond to his clues and hints. He seems to live inside those games."

Stan scrolled through the past several weeks' postings and turned on her printer. "Let's print out all his notes and see what we have. Maybe we can profile him from his notes. Make him our very own adventure game."

Chapter Two

Lulie Billingsley decided to go ahead with her party in spite of her cold. Every one of the junior class at Benchley had been passing around this monster cold. Since yesterday morning, Stan's eyes had been red pinpoints. Her hair hung in hanks. She swore that she wouldn't have gone to Lulie's party even if she'd been in perfect health, so she certainly wasn't going to go looking like a poster person for sinus medication.

When Lulie called to invite me, she broke into a coughing fit. Barking like a seal into the phone, she asked if I wanted to bring a date.

"I don't have anyone to bring at the moment, unless you want one of my mom's retreads."

"I don't have an unending supply of boys, you know," she snapped.

"Ever the gracious hostess," I murmured.

The thing about Lulie's parties is that no one looks forward to them and everybody goes to them. Lulie's older brother Jack is the main draw. The instant you begin to wonder why you came to another of Lulie's numbing parties, he and his band of college friends suddenly appear in the living room as if they've been beamed down from Starship *Enterprise*.

The Rinehart twins will be there, Carl and Mark. One of them is a lacrosse star. Their father is in city politics, so they have the use of a black city-owned car, which they park illegally all over town. Both have the shiny-eyed, alert look that one connects with places other than New York. Lulie expects us to act excited when they arrive, as if she were Monte Hall and they were extraordinary prizes. Stan calls them Biff and Whiff, the Good Sports.

I went down to Stan's loft the night before the party to cheer her up. She was sitting at the computer, typing away, muttering under her breath. The screen filled up with words. She didn't even glance up at me. "Sit down. I'm talking to some guy in Chicago. He's one of the founders of the Funhouse board. I want to download some of their fantasy-game files onto my board."

"What are you wearing to Lulie's?"

"They have an interesting pattern of access codes to assure they don't have feds hacking onto their board. The guy shared his program with me for bumping someone off your board. I'm writing interesting programs with other sysops. You drop secret little control sequences into your program that scramble the data of anyone poking around your board who shouldn't be. I bet Freddy Frobisher would love to get his hands on a code this heavy."

"I'm wearing my wine-colored slacks and sweater."

"I haven't heard from Mr. Rogers in two days. He hasn't even posted on the board. I checked Funhouse and Adam's Apple, but he hasn't checked onto those, either. Lately he's been posting all over the place. Then suddenly he disappears. I hope the kid isn't sick or something. He's never missed one of our dates before."

Dates? I thought to myself. How can she call talking to someone over a computer screen a date? I didn't say anything, though, because Stan's become extra-touchy about being a sysop. No jokes about her board or about the users.

"More and more, the users who call want to chat with the old sysop," Stan said. "One guy who called last night says he tried three times last week to get me. He was about to give up when he tried one last time this afternoon. Good thing I came straight home from school. We got to talking about cracking. I'm still not sure I want to allow it on my board. If you're going to be a sysop, you have to devote yourself to the system. If they can't get you online, they'll dial another board."

"Do you want to spend the night at my house?" I asked her.

Stan looked up at me, amazed. "What did I just say? I have to be here. I'm the sysop."

"Think maybe you're carrying this thing too far? You can't chain yourself to the computer." I replied. "Lulie may be a dud, but there are going to be live boys at her party. No blips on a screen. Have you forgotten about real people?"

"Whiff and Biff? Ride around in their dumb car and park in a bus stop? That sounds like a great evening."

"Why do you have to run everything down?"

Stan sneezed and reached for a tissue. "I'll be too sick to go."

"That would work with my mom, but yours would encourage you to go to the Arctic with a chest infection. For a beach party."

Stan laughed. "With some foul herb brew from her Indian nutritionist tucked into my parka. I don't want to go. None of those guys wants to go out with me. Lulie invites me so she can use you as a lure to get top-quality boys to show up."

I sneezed and looked around desperately for tissues. "That's nonsense. You're feeling sorry for yourself because you have a cold." I blew my nose a few times and collapsed on the bed. "Maybe I won't go to the party, either. We can nurse each other back to health."

Stan's face softened. "Okay, I'll go. And I'll spend the night at your house afterward. I'll close the board for the night. But don't expect this to be a regular occurrence."

"I think you should wear your black jersey dress with the batwing sleeves."

Stan smiled and shook her head. "For Lulie's parties, one has to dress very sensibly. I shall braid my hair in those tiny Bo Derek braids and—" Stanwyck sneezed a few times and wiped her damp red eyes on her sleeve. "What difference does it make? Nobody's going to be looking at me, anyway."

Stanwyck's selection of clothes for the party showed that she'd dressed with a fever. She was wearing a fur-trimmed sweater of her mother's and a suede skirt that had about two pounds of lint on it. Her hair was in tiny braids, but instead of falling straight, the braids were kind of skewed to the side, giving her the appearance of recent electrocution. "You look great, Stan," I said a bit too fiercely.

"My inner voice has been telling me all afternoon to go to bed with hot tea and aspirin, but I couldn't miss one of Lulie's parties. All those cute little hot dogs and pink potato salad."

Since my parents had a dinner date across town, they dropped us off at the party on their way. Each time Mom caught my eye in the elevator, she squinted her eyes in a secretive way as though we shared a joke. Dad was answering Stan's questions about the computer configuration they had at his office.

"Coming home, you girls wait for Walter Billingsley to put you in a cab. And call us when you're leaving their apartment." Mom gave out these instructions automatically. "If it's not too late," she added, handing me a folded ten-dollar bill.

"We'll be fine," I said, slipping the bill into the top of my boot. Emergency money. If I ever called Mom after midnight, she'd have heart failure, but it makes her feel better to insist we call.

The party was in full swing. Most of the girls in our class were there. Several boys from St. Benedict's were gathered around the new girl, Sabrina Waters. She had radar that drew every guy in the metropolitan area. Lulie must have noticed Sabrina's magic, too. She had been hanging all over Sabrina for the past two weeks.

As we hung up our coats, Stan pointed to Sabrina. "I knew she'd attract them like a magnet."

"How did you know that?"

"She wouldn't have a name like Sabrina if she sat in the corner looking at her hands."

"How are you, Jess? Want to check out Lulie's new tapes?" Carl Rinehart flashed me his well-scrubbed smile.

"You have any idea what kind of computer your dad uses in his office?" Stan asked without looking up.

Carl shrugged. "A big one. Coming, Jess?"

About half an hour later, I looked up from dancing with Carl's twin, Mark. Stan was sitting in the corner looking at her hands. "Want to investigate that mountain of food I saw in the kitchen?" Mark asked when the music stopped.

"Why not ask Stanwyck?"

"I pass. She'll grill me about computers. I know you two are tight, but she's a real one-note."

"Haven't you ever been utterly involved in something, wanted to know everything you could about a subject?" I asked him.

"She's obsessed."

"You're a total turkey." I walked over to Stan. "Want some food?"

"What happened to you and the Gee-Whiz Twins?"

"Stan, it's a party. We're here to have a good time." I felt as if I were the demilitarized zone between Stan and the world.

Lulie hurried toward us, holding the hand of a tall, red-haired guy wearing a Donald Duck sweatshirt. I was smiling before they reached us. "Jess, this is Jack's roommate, Jack!"

"Really?"

"Makes for wonderful confusion on our corridor," he said. "Whenever some guy shouts 'Jack, you miserable worm,' I

24

figure they must mean him. And whenever someone says 'Jack, there's a dynamite-sounding girl on the phone,' I know they mean me."

A couple of explosive sneezes burst out behind me.

"This is my friend Stanwyck Baum," I said to Jack.

Lulie frowned. "You probably should have stayed home with that cold."

"She wanted to, Lulie. It was the cold who insisted on coming." I turned to Jack. "Stan and I were about to invade the kitchen. Join us?"

"There's enough food in here to feed the Ethiopian children for a year," Stan said, rolling up some slices of turkey around a warty pickle.

"Let's not think about starvation while we're pigging out." Jack was piling inches of cold cuts onto a hero roll. "Is there any cheese down your way, Jess?"

I handed him a plate with sliced cheddar and Swiss cheese. "What are you studying at Columbia?"

"Prelaw. My dad's a lawyer. My grandad's a lawyer."

"How original." Stan flopped down, shoulders sagging. "No need for me to eat any of this mess." She surveyed her plate sadly. "Can't taste anything." She rubbed her red-tipped nose.

"How attractive." Jack put his arm around me and firmly led me toward the door. "Let's find a secluded spot to eat our chow. You can tell me all the secrets of your life."

We settled into Lulie's room and were joined by Sabrina and the Rinehart twins. Both were competing for Sabrina's attention. Carl hovered so close to her ear whispering little jokes that their faces seemed to melt together. Mark kept running back to the kitchen for more ice, more soda, more

25

napkins, asking Sabrina did she want apple pie, cookies, all the while casting dagger looks at his twin.

"I've got to make a call," she said, easing herself out of Mark's grasp. "My mom. I told her I'd call before eleven."

I leaned over to Jack and whispered "The twins're getting ready to pull her in half, like a toy."

"Maybe we should Xerox her and settle the dispute."

I liked Jack's robust laugh. He had a real easy manner, as if he saw life as a long sunlit country road stretching in front of him and he had all the time in the world to get where he was going.

A couple kids drifted in with Wendy Cartright behind them. "Quick, close the door!" one of them shouted.

"She'll track us down and run off at the mouth about computers no matter where we are. What's wrong with that girl?" another said.

Wendy looked up and saw me sitting on the floor. "Sorry, Jess, but Stanwyck is too much. She's numbing everybody out with this computer talk. Who cares about her stupid bulletin board?"

"No one in this tribe—that's for sure," complained a guy I didn't know. "Only nerds go in for that hacking business. At our school only the geekiest would even admit to fanatical keyboarding the way she does."

"Some of the fantasy games are fun," Jack said. "One of my roommates last year, a hacker named Ian, made a good piece of change writing an interactive adventure game. The player has to tell the computer which direction he wants to go over the bridge, then he falls in quicksand, and he has to decide how to wriggle out before the sandworms eat him. I never paid much attention, but that's the general idea."

Stanwyck was standing in the doorway. "Those games are a dime a dozen. They're random-shot games, timewasters. There's no rhyme or reason for why you go to the left or the right, or climb the tree or cross the bridge. The real challenges are games that use logic. You have several items— like a match, a piece of paper, maybe a key—and you have to decide when to use them. It's like chess. You develop a plan and execute it step by step."

At the sound of her voice a pall fell over the room. My heart ached for her. I tried to telegraph a signal to cut her monologue short, but Stan's like a washing machine that's got to go through the whole cycle. Painfully, I listened while everyone shifted and began whispering to each other. Stan seemed unaware of the effect she was having.

"There are esoteric variations of dungeons and dragons that have been going for a year on some of the game boards. Real serious competitions. I get requests on my board all the time for help with Zork, Enchanter, Starcross. It's the responsibility of the sysop to keep all the hints and game strategies current.

"Which reminds me, have any of you ever played Planetfall or a new one called Lucifer's Realm? I need someone who can keep hints for those games updated on the board. I've lucked out, found a guy who knows Hitchhiker clues—it's surreal. He's probably the New York *expert* on the Galaxy strategy. He used to be part of the Adventurer's Tavern board system, but he's exclusive with the Headboard now. He thinks I run the best small board in the country. His handle is Mr. Rogers, a real heavy role-player."

"And now a word from our sponsor," said Carl, fiddling

with the tips of Sabrina's golden hair. He looked as if he had no intention of leaving the room again.

Stanwyck raised her voice. "There are other kinds of games, more realistic ones, like Asylum—"

"That sounds like one you'd be good at, Stanwyck."

"They let you out of the laughing academy tonight? Or were the guards asleep when you tried to cross the bridge with your match and enchanter?"

"Three weeks in the rubber room, zonko!"

I stood up, fueled by the confusion on Stan's face. "Don't knock it till you've tried it. I thought those games were off the wall, too, until I played on Stan's computer for a few hours. You get so involved, you draw yourself a little map and imagine falling down the ravine, now how do you get yourself out—"

"Pull the plug!" Sabrina called out.

"Let me take you home," Jack said softly. "What you're trying to do is not working."

"Stan's staying overnight," I told him.

"Then I'll take both of you home." He smiled and squeezed my hand. "Don't look so tragic. It's only a party, and not a very good one at that."

At the door Lulie handed me my coat. "Good night, and thanks for bringing Partybuster with you."

"You really are a swine, Lulie Billingsley." Coughing dramatically, Stan swept out of the apartment like a movie star, trailing a roll of toilet paper to the elevator.

Stanwyck was glum the next morning. When I woke up, she was furtively watching me from behind the book she was reading. Lying in bed surrounded by damp tissues that looked like dead butterflies, she was a disaster area. She threw her book to the floor and sighed mournfully. "I'm the nerd of the class, the wonk, the geek, and all because I've hooked into technology."

I rolled over and pretended to go back to sleep, but Stanwyck kept talking. "I like understanding how things work. I like being able to control the programs I write. It's thrilling to know the system so well, from the and/or gates through the flipflops, the machine language, the assembler, and up into the interpreted languages—"

"Ground to Stanwyck. I have no idea what you're talking about. Could you break it down into simple English?"

Stan kicked off her covers and sat on the edge of my bed. "That's why I need to talk on the boards. The guys understand what I'm saying. And they get as excited as I do over cracking a new piece of code. It's not as much fun if you can't share it."

"But Stan, I've never been a math wizard like you. Just walking into the math room, with those odd symbols and equations all over the board, gives me a queasy feeling, like I'm falling into a deep hole."

"I've always loved science courses. From the time I was a tiny kid, every time one of those space shots went up, I'd think to myself, I want to learn to do that. Those are the people in charge."

"In charge of what?" I cried.

"Mapping."

"Stanwyck, I'm trying to understand," I growled. "Talk normal."

"Mapping which way we'll go with technology, what kind of society we'll be."

I felt as if it was all over my head. "I don't see how you get all that stuff from playing Enchanter games over telephone lines."

"The games are proof of where your head is at, what kind of hacker you are, not an end in themselves. You see, Jess, you buy one of these games, then you learn how to hack out the program code. Suppose the rules of the game say you have four alien crew on your spaceship, and when they're destroyed, you are dead. You change the code to give yourself an unlimited supply of aliens. Then you can never die. Your ship is safe no matter how long you play the game."

"So that's being in charge." I put on my robe and went to the kitchen for breakfast. I was grateful when Lulie called to gossip about the party. We must have talked half an hour but Stan didn't appear in the kitchen. Figuring her cold was getting the better of her, I fixed her some tea and toast and carried it back to my room.

"Guess what," I said, putting the tray on the table next to her. "Sabrina has a date tonight with both twins."

"She's an airhead. Calling her mom in the middle of a party," Stan grumbled. "I hear her mom picks Sabrina up most afternoons after school. Maybe delicious Sabrina can't find her way through the complicated subway system."

"Just because she's beautiful doesn't mean she's stupid." I squinted angrily. "She's in advanced English and French."

"And she dropped physics."

"I didn't even attempt physics. Am I an airhead?"

"Of course not. Let's not fight. I feel miserable." She reached for the box of tissues to grab my sympathy. "Sabrina doesn't need me to protect her. With a face like hers, she'll glide through life. Face it, Jess. If she had been a real bow-wow new kid coming in in the middle of the year, Lulie wouldn't have invited her over to wash the dishes."

I swallowed my annoyance and decided to try again. "Lulie says Jack's going to ask me out. Isn't that super?"

"I thought he was as appealing as cold fried eggs."

"Because he doesn't sit at a computer all day bragging about his phreaking exploits to people he'll never see?"

"Because he doesn't know anything about anything."

"You said five words to him. What's wrong with you?"

"I have a cold."

"I hope that's it," I said, escaping into the shower.

Chapter Three

"Going out with a college guy is hardly the ultimate double bucky shanghai." As soon as we returned to the loft, Stan began scrolling through the messages that had been posted on the Headboard while we were shopping. "You'd better not turn into one of those giggling airheads, Jess Graham."

"Jack's more fun than baby-sitting a video screen." I'd failed to coax her away from the computer that morning. Finally Mrs. Baum had decided all BBS and no life was making her daughter gray and odd.

"Go out and spend money. Buy some bizarre teen-age clothes or ear-splitting teen-age records. Let me despair of you the way mothers are supposed to. Locking yourself up in that room, captive to that nasty little screen, is no life. You have no color in your face."

"Seems like you've got enough to despair over without my

buying punk clothes," Stanwyck observed. "But I'll super-vise Jess. Who knows what will occur when the world of the preppie collides with unnatural fibers?"

We'd gone to the SoHo record store, but Stan had sighed and tapped her foot while I looked through the new releases. When I suggested we stop for lunch, she dragged me into one of those stand-up hot-dog stands. Clearly she was not in the mood for a leisurely day. Knowing when to admit defeat, we went back to the loft so she could reconnect with the board.

"Jack's coming over tonight. He's bringing a couple Bette Davis movies. He's got a humongous library of videotaped movies. Why don't you come over, too?"

"Afraid to be alone with Joe College?"

"Don't be such a prune, Stan. He's neat. No other guy would hang out with my mother voluntarily. He came over two nights last week. He seems comfortable even playing Scrabble with her and Dad."

"Did he mention how she cheats with that pocket dictio-nary on her lap?"

"No, he's a gentleman. As a matter of fact, he let her win."

"Must be true love." Stanwyck glanced at me sideways.

"Don't be a fool. I just met him a couple weeks ago," I said supercasually. I knew if I admitted how much I liked Jack, I'd get more of the chilly disapproval that's become Stan's specialty.

"Look at this post—it's from Mr. Rogers: 'Call voice immediately.' "

"What else would you call with? Feet?"

34

"*Voice* means over the phone, personally, not using the modem and the computer."

"You mean the way we civilians from the dark ages communicate?"

Stan switched off the modem. "He gave me his number last week. His actual phone number. We've talked a couple times. Not through the board. That means he likes me as a person, not merely as a sysop." She brushed her hair off her forehead. "You want some tea or something to eat?"

"You want to make this call *privately*?" I could hardly contain myself. Stan seemed blind to the fact that Mr. Rogers was a wimp using the handle of a kids' TV program. He was probably eight years old.

"He goes to Tech. His name is Noah Kurtz, and he's no wimpy kid." She could always read my mind. "Remember, I've been talking to him for a couple months. He's brilliant. He's devised some of the best game cheats on the boards."

"That business where you make sure the spaceship never runs short of ammo, no matter how many times you've been hit?"

"The point is, he can hack out their codes and find that piece of hex or machine code and change it. That takes megasmarts." She put on fresh lip gloss and reached for the telephone. "You have your Jack-in-the-box, I have my machine wizard."

I went into the kitchen and pulled a container of last night's Chinese takeout from the refrigerator.

A few minutes later Stan joined me. "You know the kid even set up a game-cheat menu. You can choose your option, depending on which game you're playing. Infinite bullets, infinite supply of men or magic potions, nobody dies.

He's got a real gift for this sort of thing." She picked up a fork and began poking through the cold food, skewering the cashews and tossing aside the chicken. "I'm going to ask him to help me add more fantasies to the board. He knows them all. We could make this the best board on the eastern seaboard. I've needed a partner in BBS for a while now. Since you don't seem to care about it."

"What did he want?"

"I invited him over, and he's coming." She turned to me, her face flushed. "I thought he'd say no."

"He's probably been angling for an invitation. Dropping hints that you never picked up on. Sometimes you can be pretty dense, Stan. You guys have been talking for months. He knows how sharp you are from your notes. And you know more about computers and bulletin boards and all that downloading business than anyone else. Remember, even that Freddy Frobisher was impressed with the kind of board you run. And he's supposed to be the best in the business. Why shouldn't this clown want to meet you?"

"There's going to be a problem." Her face cracked into misery. "When he gets here, about an hour from now, he's going to realize I lied. He's only coming because I told him I had hotshot connections with this board in Oklahoma that is famous for cracking fantasy software, and he's hot to download the newest ware for his collection. Since I don't have any decent cracked programs on the board yet—"

"How come?"

"It's not exactly legal. Some nonsense about copyright laws, although it seems foolish to me. You can tape records and give them to your friends, so why can't you copy software and give the programs to your friends? It's not like Tim Mooney, trying to make money off friends."

"You sound like Freddy Frobisher. Want to end up riding the high school circuit on behalf of the feds? Scaring kids?"

"It's Freddy's friends on the Funhouse board who post the buckiest cracked ware. They post lists to me every few days, offering swaps, and I post back to them, saying as soon as I have some new programs, we'll download to each other. I left old Freddy a couple messages. So far no answer. He was kind of cute, wasn't he?"

"I don't remember."

"Old Jack Sprat's wiped everyone else's face out of your databank, right?" Stan grinned. "I better not rag you until we see what Noah Kurtz looks like."

"Hope he's tall enough to reach the doorbell."

Stan tossed the empty food container into the garbage, licked the fork clean, and put it back in the drawer. "What am I going to tell him? About getting him here under false pretenses."

"Did it ever occur to you he may want to see you more than he wants to get his hands on your cracked software? He may be as curious about you—"

"Thank you, Ann Landers." Her tone scoffed, but she looked pleased.

Stan changed her clothes four times. She settled on an old knit pullover of her father's, worn back to front, sneakers without laces, and very old jeans. I felt like Miss Congeniality in a Miss Grub contest.

When the buzzer rang, Stan reached for a pair of large plastic heart-shaped sunglasses and said, "Remember, he's mine."

Noah Kurtz was about thirteen years old, thin, pale, and spindly. Squint-eyed, thin-lipped, he looked as if smiling were against his religion. He came in, took off his gray old-man coat and never went beyond hello. Stan took off her glasses, chewed on the frames, and made a face at me behind the kid's back.

He reached into his coat pocket and pulled out a disk that he then handed to Stan. The way someone else would produce candy. "I didn't have time to print it out. It's got my Hitchhiker files on it. You can study them so you'll be able to run the hint section yourself."

Stan flew around the room, turning on the stereo, offering Coke and cookies. Did he like ZZ Top? Would he like to hear the new Springsteen album? "Or my own new hit single? Hot data?" She refused to look at me.

"The system," he said without expression. "I'm here to check out your system." He reminded me of a doctor making a house call.

"Where do you live, Noah?" I asked.

"With my father," he answered impatiently. His tone said this was not a social call. He seemed wary of appearing pleasant.

Silently we trooped into the bedroom and Stan booted the system. Noah sat at the keyboard and stared at the screen. As the program came up, his hands hovered over the keyboard like a pianist in the first moments of a concert. He scrolled through the past week of posted messages, grunting but making no comments. Stan fidgeted with the stack of disks, casting me helpless looks now and then. I wondered that she hadn't picked up on the kid's weirdness from their

38

voice conversations. No way he sounded like anything other than what he was—a humorless, know-it-all fledgling hacker.

"Guess I'll be getting on home," I said cheerfully.

"Not yet," implored Stan. "Help me get rid of him," she whispered.

"Got to go," I insisted. Noah didn't look up from the screen. As he flipped from one section of the board to another, he nodded and chuckled to himself. Stan and I might have been transported to another city.

I reached for my jacket, and Stan followed me to the door. "How can I get rid of the little turd?"

"He's a real epsilon."

"He does know all those games." Stan reversed direction. "He's phenomenal. It's as if the clues were actually in his hands, wired into the nerve endings in his fingers. He's played them all. And that's what the members of the board want to know about. Hints, clues, like that."

"What's the fun in sysoping a board for the likes of Noah and his friends? It's a service project. You should be getting extra credit at school, the way we do when we work at the hospital or at the home for brain-damaged kids. Stan's own special olympics for nerdish hackers."

"Cut it out. I didn't realize how young the kid was. I like those games, and I figured the people who logged on my board were like me. Look at Freddy Frobisher. He's no baby-faced nerd. Guess I'll have to get into cracking. That's where the cool guys are."

"Hey, Archangel, your board's ringing," called Noah. "Some guy wants the sysop. You want to answer or let it go?"

She couldn't resist. "Don't go yet, Jess. I'll be right back," she called over her shoulder.

I buttoned my coat and pulled on my gloves. "Jess, come quick! It's Freddy! He's on the board." Stan was laughing with delight, the embarrassment of Noah bleeped off the screen. "I knew he'd call. It was just a matter of time. Patience is a virtue."

She set the system to record the conversation with Freddy on disk. "So I can read it slowly later," she said shyly. Then she turned back to the board and was concentrating so intently on the screen that she seemed to have crawled inside the computer.

"He says there's a hot new BBS out of Omaha that he's been posting through. By routing his board through theirs, the feds won't be able to track him. They've got a tap on his phone lines, but he dumps all his files through this Omaha board. Isn't that brilliant? He thinks we can create the hottest board in the country if we unite—his board in Minneapolis, mine here, and his Funhouse friends in Chicago."

I stood in the doorway watching Stan laugh and jump around while she typed answers to Freddy. As his words ran across the screen, Stan got more and more excited. Poor clunky Noah backed away from the computer as if it had become a villain.

"We have to use the same software for all three boards. Since yours is the most up-to-date package, you download your board-management program to me and Charlie. It would never do for us to go online running old software if we're going to be the best pirate board in the whole U.S.A."

"Pirate boards are illegal," Noah said in his nasal voice.

"Don't you have to get home?" Stan snapped.

"We'll be joint sysops. We'll run under your handle if you want."

"He's trying to use you as a cover, Stan."

"I'm going to be famous. We'll have the buckiest board, and we're going to offer the newest ware. There's nothing wrong with it. All we do is crack the copy-protection code, like cracking a combination lock, lift the lock-up code from the program, and distribute it to crackers. Nobody gets hurt. Half the crackers don't ever run the ware they collect. It's just nice to have it. It's a hobby. Don't believe all that legal jargon. It's only swapping. The feds should spend their time running after real crooks and leave us alone."

Noah put on his coat. "I thought you were interested in the challenge of fantasy games. But this pirating business, that's what gives phreakers and hackers a bad name," he said.

"Control-z, twerp. We're collecting ware, not pirating to sell it."

Stan signed off with Freddy after promising to download her sysop program to him that evening. "Eight o'clock, I have a date with Freddy!" She looked happier than she had in weeks.

"I thought we were going to work on Ultima together," whined Noah.

"Good-bye, Noah," Stan said gaily. "In case you hadn't noticed, we're in SoHo, not in one of your Enchanter fantasies. This loft is not a locked room. You can find your way out more easily than from Asylum. No key, no note to the guard. No clues required. Just *go!*"

He looked at her for a moment, then took off his coat, folded it neatly on the chair, and sat down. "You've been running a good board. Lots of us use it regularly. So I'm going to program the time to download some data on you." He folded his hands. "Cracking isn't illegal like the feds

41

insist. You're right. But these guys are going to let you take the fall when the feds trace the phreak. I've heard they take kids they've caught and force them to hack out our codes, that they even keep track of our handles. They have clever ways of getting to the heart of any phreak. And who cares if you're right? They have the power. They can come to this house and impound your equipment."

"I don't need the advice of a twelve-year-old." Stan eyed him coldly. "Talking online to you, I thought you were like me. But I was wrong. Freddy is like me. He wants to do a board together. Don't you get it? We're going to have the best system in the country. I've written a program for multiusers that'll revolutionize bulletin boards. This is no fantasy game."

"You're right, this is no fantasy game," he said. "Because in games, there's no place to hide yourself in somebody else's board. You have to play the next move, taking the next step. It's your mind against the machine."

"I never get involved in those games, Noah. Remember, you provided me with the clues. I liked being the sysop. Running the board, talking to people all night long. You game phreaks get so *intense*. Swapping ideas and pieces of code is where it's at for me."

"No disagreement. Sometimes I'm online all night long. You get to typing answers so fast online, you forget you're typing. Sometimes it's like a Vulcan mind meld—you feel that you're doing exactly what Spock does on *Star Trek*."

Stan nodded and sat on the kitchen counter, swinging her legs. "I shouldn't have told you I had all those cracked games for you. I was wrong to lead you on. Sorry I was such a worm. I thought it would be double bucky to meet you."

42

Noah ran his stubby fingers through his hair. "I'm not good at talking in person. I prefer talking online. You can plan what you have to say, control how long you talk. Sometimes I work on a game for twenty hours, sleep a few hours, then back to the console. I get so involved in the game, I don't need to eat, I don't need anyone. It's myself and the machine. That's the beauty of the games. That's how real phreakers are. I thought you were a dedicated phreaker. That's why I could talk to you."

Stan had nodded sympathetically while Noah was talking. It wasn't like her to be so mean. She's only vicious to people who are strong. And this kid clearly had the toughness of cooked macaroni.

"Thanks for your help, Mr. Rogers. I couldn't have kept up with all the postings without your clues these last couple of months. Maybe you should start your own fantasy board. Then you could keep current with the contacts you've made on the Headboard. I'll give you all my disks of postings for the past few months. Since we won't be doing fantasy anymore." Stan danced around the living room in a graceless gallop. "Maybe Freddy will come up with a super new name for the board. Not like those silly Pirate's Cove types. So obvious."

"But you're doing this for Freddy, not for the fun of the phreak, and that's cheating." Noah's voice had risen to a squeak. He cleared his throat and shook his head wearily. He looked like a little old man. "You don't have to turn your board over to the pirates."

"Thanks for the clue," Stan said, reaching for her sunglasses.

Noah turned to me. "Do you phreak?"

I felt so sorry for him. "Mostly I help Stanwyck with the

43

postings. So I know how much help you've been to her. She couldn't have provided those game hints without you. She doesn't know the right moves the way you do."

He stifled a yawn. For the first time I noticed the deep circles under his eyes. "Got up at four to get online with the wizard master. I had to get four bags of gold from the paladin before school." The hurt was clear on his face.

"Maybe if I followed some of your clues, I could learn," I said.

"Of course you could. That's why a good board is so important. It teaches people how to program, how to phreak, how to play the games." His forehead was creased with earnestness. "You know how nice it is, sitting in your room, talking online, no sweat because they're people you'll never have to face. You know the person is like you, and that they like things exactly the way you do." He burst into tears. "I never should have come here." He pushed past me and ran through the door.

"Let him go," Stan said.

"You've turned heartless," I shouted, and ran after Noah. But when I got down to the street, there was no sign of him.

Chapter Four

My life is beginning to play like an Afterschool Special. Each day I come home from school, and around five, begin watching the clock, surprised when the phone rings on schedule. Jack calls when he finishes work in the college bookstore. The way we try so hard to make each other laugh is very TV. Knowing how much Stan disapproves of all things reeking of sitcoms and what she calls the Valentine mentality, I have kept a lot of the Jack business to myself. When I want to talk to someone about Jack, it's usually Lulie, who was born with a TV remote control in her mouth.

Stan is not secretive about her alliance with Freddy Frobisher. He's been posting announcements of their hot new board on BBS all over the country. I'd sure like to see what his phone bill looks like. He calls Stanwyck at three in the morning, when the rates are cheapest, and downloads hours of files to her. Her eyes are looking very sunken these days, and her face long and pointy.

Lulie and I were finishing lunch yesterday when Stan came into the cafeteria. She slammed her tray down next to mine and flopped into the chair. "Did you ever hear anything so outrageous as that history assignment? No way it can be done without hours in the library."

"The purpose of the assignment is to get us to use the library," said Lulie, pulling out her mirror and lipstick.

"Right, genius. But the library is not in my house. And I have to stick close to home these days. Remember that gorgeous guy who spoke in assembly last month? The one the feds had on a short leash? Well, we're connected with miles of cables. Very intimate."

"Is that why your eyes are so smudgy and dark? At first I thought it was makeup, but Jess reminded me you don't use makeup." Lulie flashed a smile. "So it must be natural."

"How are things going with the new board?" I asked hurriedly. "Have you heard from Noah?"

Stanwyck shot me her traitor look and said nothing.

"I was thinking about Noah yesterday. Wondering how he was going to survive without your board." I turned to Lulie. "These hackers—you know, kids whose whole lives are their computers—have grown to depend on Stanwyck's bulletin board."

Lulie frowned. "It's unhealthy, spending all their time with a machine, never developing friends. Of course if they had friends to begin with, they wouldn't develop these sicko relationships with machines. They'd be too busy."

I felt as if I were a rope being yanked in two directions. "Stan is friends with the people she meets phreaking. That's

46

the whole point. Making friends with people who like what you like. No more weird than hanging out on the tennis courts."

Stanwyck ripped the cover off her straw. "As a matter of fact, I was planning to go to Astoria this afternoon to see old Noah. I copied some disks for him so he can set up his own fantasy board. Why don't you come with me?" She slouched in her chair, a look of challenge on her face. "Since you like him so much."

"Jess and I are going shopping this afternoon," Lulie replied.

"We can shop another day," I said firmly. I was eager to get solid again with Stanwyck, and if trekking out to see Noah was the price, I was willing to pay it. "I'd love to visit Noah." She wouldn't admit it, but she must have been feeling wormy for the way she'd treated the kid when he'd come to her house.

"Good. I'm not absolutely sure where he lives, but it's in Astoria and the name is Kurtz. How hard can it be?"

We matched the phone number with an address in the phone book and set off. It felt good to be on an adventure with Stan again. She seemed pleased too, winking as she pointed out weird people on the subway.

We got off the train and asked directions from a man in a bakery. Eating cream doughnuts, we walked three blocks until we saw a beauty salon with a yellow canopy. "We turn down here and walk two blocks. Then it's on the right." Stan offered me another doughnut.

"No thanks, I'm about sugared out. Jack is a chocolate freak, so we're always having cocoa and eclairs. He's crazy about eclairs."

Stan looked thoughtful. "I don't know what Freddy likes

47

to eat. He has a super phreak going. We can talk voice for hours, and it doesn't cost a cent. We talked until four o'clock this morning." Her face broke into a grin. "He told me about this girl he knew who was a sysop but couldn't take the pressure. Guys were posting foul letters on her board, and she got totally bummed out."

"Does that ever happen to you."

"Guys occasionally leave crummy notes. I erase them. It doesn't do any good to keep their names on file because worms like that call with different names each time, so you can't program the board to disconnect them when they log on."

"Isn't this the building, 115-34?"

We had to ring the buzzer three times. "It's Stanwyck Baum, I've brought you some files," she shouted through the intercom several times before we were buzzed into the building. The hallways reeked of fried food. Tonight's dinner being cooked behind closed doors added a fresh layer of smell. The Kurtz apartment was on the sixth floor. The paint was chipped in the elevator and in the hallways. The doors and walls were painted an institutional dark gray. The window at the end of the hall was so grimy, there was barely enough light to find the apartment.

"Look, Stan, that door is cracked open."

We hurried toward the apartment. "Hey, Noah, is that you?" There was a chain across the door.

"What are you two doing here?" he asked through the door.

"We came to bring you some files," I answered.

"Just hand 'em through the door. I got no time for visitors."

"We won't stay long." I moved closer to the crack in the door.

"I'm waiting to download some help files from a guy in Tennessee who's been working the new Pit game. He'll be home from school any minute. They're an hour behind us." It was dark in the apartment. I couldn't see Noah's face.

"Give us a couple minutes. We brought you some doughnuts. I want to apologize for being such an epsilon the other day." Stan moved in front of the crack in the door. "I was on a tear. Somebody must have crashed my central i/o device during the night."

He grunted and opened the door. "I was working on Sorcerer entries. Why didn't I see it before? After you open the locked room with the brass key, you can take the ten-pound note and pay for a lantern from the dwarf. Once you have the lantern, you can read the note—that's what's always stopped me. How to read the note. Because there are no candles."

"Speaking of candles, do you have any lamps here? Or do we have to find the dwarf first?" We were standing in a dark hall. There were no lights in the living room.

Noah seemed surprised by the request. "I never turn lights on. It casts glare on the screen."

"Must be nice for your mother," I said, squinting my eyes to get a sense of the room in which we were standing. "Stumbling around her house in the dark."

"She's dead," he said without feeling.

"Oh, I'm so sorry," I cried.

"No big deal."

There were stacks of books all over the floor in the living room. It looked as if the tenants were either moving out or moving in. The table where they must have eaten their meals had a couple of dirty coffee cups on it. More books with papers stuffed into them were piled up near the dishes.

"Can we see your system?" Stan said to cover our embarrassment.

The walls of Noah's room were covered with hand-drawn maps. In some places three or four maps were pinned on top of each other. His computer sat on a long skinny table facing the wall. It had probably been a kitchen table. There were no chairs, no pictures, no bureau—nothing standard except a mattress on the floor covered with a faded quilt and a pillow. Several clipboards were nailed to the wall next to the mattress, about a foot off the floor.

"There's this new Pit game on several elite BBS. It's called Dark Spell. I'm hoping they'll name me a Wizard Guide on the Funhouse."

"Hey, Noah, I'm tight with the Funhouse sysop. I'll tell him to appoint you a wizard." Stan turned to me and said in a low melodramatic tone, "You are searching for treasure in a great pit. Most of those who venture into the pit never return."

"All those games sound alike to me," I said.

"That's 'cause you don't know how to play them," snapped Noah. "It's a real test of your logic skills. You're lost in a labyrinth deep within the earth, searching for a vast treasure, trying to avoid the diabolical traps. You have to play for hours to learn what the traps are. Then you have to remember where they are and how to avoid them. When people say games, they mean simple-minded. Well, try playing Dungeons or Sorcerer, and see how far you get." Noah's pale cheeks flushed as he spoke. But he never smiled. "You really know the sysop?" he asked Stan without taking a breath.

"Sure. Forgive me for being such a crumb the other day, and I'll log on to Funhouse tonight. But the guy you were so against is one of the sysop's best friends," Stan said slyly. "Freddy's my connection."

"I've heard good things about him. He does great game cheats," admitted Noah. "He used to post tutorials on not getting caught and intricate tricks around the feds." Stan burst out laughing.

"What's a game cheat?" A glance at the clock told me it was time for Jack to be calling. I couldn't believe that I was stuck in this drafty bedroom, sitting on the cold floor, watching a flickering computer screen with a mole-eyed kid, when I could have been talking to Jack.

"They caught him and made him dead meat," Noah replied implacably. He could say the most outrageous things in his flat unaccented voice. No highs or lows. Just like the small iridescent symbols he typed so quickly onto the screen.

"What's a game cheat?" I repeated.

"A phreaker who goes into the binary part of a program and changes the codes."

"You want to run that by me in English?"

"Actually, Jess, the codes are in hex. Hexidecimal."

Stanwyck gave me her eyebrows-raised superior look. "We've been over this hundreds of times. Where's your head these days? Game cheats hack program code so that they can alter how the game's played. For instance, in one game you always fall into the quicksand and get eaten by the sandworms. Well, you find out the code for that area of the game and delete the sandworms."

51

I stood up and looked at some of the printed-out messages tacked to the wall over Noah's mattress. *I have the access number to metro guide, anyone who can crack the password, we could trade. Warning: They've got a hairy protection system* read one note. There were several complicated messages listing hints for obtaining valid credit-card numbers. One guy had inventive ways to trash dumpsters to get hold of the carbons of credit-cards transactions. *If you're caught, tell them you're looking for wires for your car. Once I tried a slick alibi, I had ripped my jacket before beginning the trash and when the guard caught me I said some guy had just mugged me and threw my wallet in here. It worked.*

"This is utterly crooked, illegal—you could go to reform school!" I cried. "Stan, tell him about Tim Mooney and his ill-fated make-a-fortune schemes." I shuddered as I remembered our own experiences trashing phone codes behind a police precinct.

"Chill out, Jess." Noah logged on to a phreaker BBS that he and Stan had been talking about. "I don't phreak credit cards. I'm not after money. I like to keep up with the talent. Listen to this guy. Risky Business is his name." In his flat nasal voice Noah read the posting as the words streamed onto the screen.

"Yours truly just wangled a job with old Ma Bell. Honest. They cleared me through. I'll be able to post zillions of firsthand inside dope for all you phreakers. The rewards will be great enough to offset the risks. Anyone with nerves of steel ready to crack tops info service. Tops is accessed through telenet. Now, who out there is ready for the big time? Remember, I'll post any codes you need from Ma Bell. Keep on phreakin'."

I must have looked appalled. Noah got up from the board and pulled on my arm. "Don't get the wrong idea, Jess. Those posts are from phreakers and carders. I don't do that. I'm a user of the boards for the fantasies. And I do a little pirating. I have a collection of about 200 games. Nothing big-time yet."

Stan nodded. "There are all different categories of BBS users. Phreakers mess with phones—you know all about them." She clutched her throat melodramatically. "And the carders are the ones who steal credit-card numbers and deserve to go to jail. Not too savory. The crackers get into program codes. They're the real brains. The pirates collect ware. It's a big network of kids all solid with each other."

"Like a crime ring," I muttered. I was uncomfortable sitting in this darkened room, listening to these postings from kids glorying in their newest methods of cracking. I suspected they were all as spidery as Noah.

"Here's an offer from a carder. *I have a ton of credit-card numbers and names. I am selling them at reasonable prices, anyone interested post to my box.*'" Noah brushed some dust from his keyboard. "I could get into carding anytime I want. I have the phone numbers of a couple secret carding boards. But I'd rather play games."

What's the difference? I wondered. The fantasy games Noah loves and the illegal phreaks are both played from kids' bedrooms. Hard to imagine a real-life federal agent bursting through your bedroom door to accuse you of criminal acts when you've been cracking program code to break some company's copy-protection scheme. All you want to do is distribute disks full of games to your friends. It seems as safe as the games you've been phreaking.

"Read this intro for the help manual for Pits, Jess. A friend of mine in Seattle wrote it. It'll grip you, pull you right in to the story," Noah said, handing me a battered sheet of paper.

I picked up the printout and carried it to the small lamp next to Noah's bed. *"Amid the half light of a guttering torch, the barbarian Breng moves quietly through the caverns,"* I read. *"Caution and stealth had aided his quest for gold. His goal: to clear the catacombs of all forms of evil creatures.*

"As a kicked pebble rattles by his side, he turns and draws his sword in one fluid motion. A quick thrust, and a lowly Anhkheg lies severed in two. Finally Breng reaches the stairs down to the next level. Although on the alert for a surprise attack, he moves down the cold stone steps. A zombie, an Ir-vile, and a doom dog all fall before his flashing sword, but not before the dog rips part of Breng's leg. Suddenly as Breng turns a corner, an undead bear attacks."

"What are you up to?" Noah asked eagerly.

"An undead bear."

"That's the beauty of Pit. Breng will be killed, his back slashed by the undead bear, but he can be resurrected to fight again. If he were totally dead, you could never pick up the game where you left off. Because you are Breng, you can always become undead."

All this talk about dead and undead sounded squirrelly. I tried to signal Stan but she was scrolling through some files.

"I've been in a teletrial," Noah told Stanwyck. "We made sure that rugwump never got near our game boards again. He can't post on any board. All the sysops are on to his game now. That's what you have to do to the spoilers. Ragwars. Want to check out some of those postings?"

"We have to leave," I said, brushing lint off my skirt. I wondered what ragwars could be. "I have a ton of homework."

"Ragwars don't solve anything," said Stan. "You can't keep a kid off a board. They come back on your board using a different name."

Noah nodded. "But they can't use their own name. It's like being dead. If you have to use a new name, you've lost your identity. You have to start all over again on the boards. If you admit you used to be called Snack Attack, and Snack Attack has been teletrialed and posted a luser, then you'll be bleeped."

"I've written code for my board that automatically disconnects any of a list of passwords I've put into the systems."

"Come on, Stan, we have to blow this fruit stand," I said, using one of Jack's favorite expressions.

She and Noah looked at me as if I were from another planet.

It's impossible to double-date with your best friend when her boyfriend hangs out over telephone lines and cracks jokes on a computer screen. That explains why I've spent the past two Saturday nights at Sabrina's house.

She's been dating both the twins, alternate weekends. She says it's no different from dating two guys, although it's kind of spooky that they look alike and act totally different.

I was getting set to go to Sabrina's house when the doorbell rang. It was Stanwyck with her knapsack. "Thought I'd surprise you. Stay the night. I've got three gallons of ice cream in my pack."

"I've got a date tonight. With Jack. I'm staying at Sabrina's."

"Again." Stan didn't seem surprised. She came in and put her pack on the floor. "Guess we better eat fast, then."

"I'm going to Sabrina's now."

"Aren't we cozy all of a sudden?"

"We're double-dating. If you had a date—"

Stanwyck jumped to her feet. "Now you have to have a date as the price of admission to see a friend. Well, news flash, Jess Graham. I have friends, too. Activity on my board is up five hundred percent. Dad's buying me a fifteen-meggie disk to accommodate all the new postings. So you and Sabrina can date all of Columbia University, for all I care. I have plenty to keep me busy."

"Is something wrong?" I asked.

Tears filled Stan's eyes. She slumped to the floor and pulled viciously at her braids. "We had a fight, we had a terrible fight."

"You and your folks?"

"No. Freddy. I had downloaded everything to him. My software and all the programs I've written for my board, so we have identical systems. I knew it was illegal to help him run a system. But he doesn't have any money after paying that federal fine, so he couldn't have been a sysop without my software and without using a cover name. Anyway, things have been going great. I have so many callers, I can barely keep up. I'm getting famous on the BBS circuit. Freddy has taught me so much about programming, he has the answers to all my technical questions. I download files to him in the middle of the night. Makes him crazy, but I'm still too chicken to use a phreaked number."

"You'd better stay chicken. I don't want to visit you in jail."

"Freddy's got this major game-cheat board going, and he

wanted to dump those data files onto my board in case the feds get wise and realize he's the Apple Tree Inspiration. If my father finds out we're cracking some of the heaviest software on the market, I'm dead meat, as Noah would say."

"So tell him no cracking menus on your board. That's elementary, my dear Stanwyck."

"I did. He reminded me game cheats and cracking are what's happening. My chirpy little postings about fantasy games are a perfect cover. His game cheaters leave their messages woven into my postings. The feds'll never pick up on it."

"He's a swine."

"I love him!" Stan wailed. "He's got a collection of almost two thousand programs, all cracked by members of the board. It's like the ultimate library of current programs. Give me a couple more weeks, I'll learn to game cheat. I called him on voice to apologize for my pruny attitude, and he called me epsilon. He reminded me of his reputation and threatened to use someone else's board if I didn't shape up."

"There's your answer. Tell him to use someone else's board."

"I'd be nowhere without him!"

"You were doing fine."

"You want me to spend my life worrying about getting undead with a bunch of wimps?"

I looked at the clock. "Could we talk about this tomorrow? I'm free all day. Right now, I have to get to Sabrina's—"

"Talk about loyal." Stanwyck rolled over on the floor and buried her face in her hands. She was still lying there when I left the house half an hour later.

Chapter Five

Whenever I see Sabrina, I'm struck by her beauty. She's not merely pretty. Her features are perfect. Great cornflower-blue eyes and long heavy blond hair, teeth white as ice—a real stereotype, but it still affects you in real life. When we're alone or with the guys, she's very funny, a super mimic. Having lived in England all those years, she speaks with a London accent.

Around her family she's silent, as if her head were somewhere else. Her parents are very reserved, the kind of adults who expect you to say yes sir and thank you ma'am as your part of the conversation. They don't even pretend to be interested in what we're doing; they ask only the most superficial questions about school. At dinner Mrs. Waters pats her lips with a corner of her damask napkin as if she were dusting a museum piece. Sabrina's stepfather is British, but he's worked all over the world training executives. Sabrina is unclear about what he trains them to do.

What people do is of great interest to *my* mother. "What do her parents do?" is always her first question. Sabrina's mother imports antiques, which she sells for a fortune. Sabrina says it's amazing how much some people are willing to shell out for a wormy old desk with warped drawers. Mom sees it differently. "With antiques a good eye is everything. Does she have a good eye, Jess?" It took all my self-control not to say, "She's got two of them, Mom." The way her mind works, Mom would load her irritation with me onto Sabrina's permanent record. Soon she'd start saying things like, "Why are you seeing so much of that girl?" With a few flicks of her tongue, Mom can turn even the most obvious princess, which Sabrina is, into a warty toad.

Sabrina and I had just convinced her mother that we wouldn't die of starvation if we didn't have any of the apple tart she'd bought for dessert. "They're especially for you girls," she'd insisted, "Clive and I don't care for sweets, but do as you like—girls always do these days." she said, when the telephone rang.

"I'll get it, Mummy."

"Tell whoever it is, we are dining. People in this country always ring up during mealtime." Mr. Waters looked put out, as if the caller were trying to bug him.

"What do your parents do when the phone rings during meals, Jess?"

"Answer it" was clearly the right answer, but not in this exam. "It bothers them, too," I assured her with a smile as smooth as cream. Why am I so willing to supply what is expected of me? Stanwyck wouldn't cave in.

Sabrina returned to the dining room and sat without saying anything.

"Who was it, darling?"

"No one. A kid from school. I said I couldn't talk."

"Who was it?" I asked. "Someone needing an assignment?"

"No one," she answered sharply.

I glanced at the untouched apple tart. Eating a piece might break the tension, but my stomach had a cramp in it. Sabrina wouldn't look at me. I wondered what I had said to bring that tight set to her lips. "Want to get ready, Sabrina? The guys will be here pretty soon."

"Where are you all going this evening?" Mrs. Waters asked as if reading from the Mother's Handbook. "I expect you home at a decent hour."

"Carl said he wanted to go to a new place, Mom, called Face Forward."

"What an odd name," murmured Mr. Waters. "Probably a disco." He said the word as if it meant "brothel."

"It's only a few blocks from here. I've been there with my parents. They have a small band, but not electric. You'd enjoy it." I flashed him my parent-taming smile.

Back in her room, Sabrina became her ordinary self. "You saved the day out there. He was about to say no Face Forward. Too bad they don't have metal, though."

"I've never been near the place, Sabrina. I was *parenting*."

She favored me with a look of pure admiration.

Carl circled the block eight times—still no parking place. "We could spend the evening in the car, getting just close enough to Face Forward to tantalize ourselves," Jack suggested.

61

"Look in the glove compartment, Sabrina. There's a sign and an electric cord. Want to give them to me?" Carl pulled in to a bus stop and parked the car in front of a fire hydrant. He took the cord that Sabrina handed him and plugged it into the cigarette lighter on the dashboard. Then he connected its other end to the sign, which flickered for a moment and then lit up: OFFICIAL CAR.

"How did you get it? Won't your father get in trouble if you use it for a very unofficial Saturday-night date?"

"My brother and I had it made up at a neon-sign shop on the West Side. It's not legitimate. But cops and meter maids assume it must be. We're never ticketed. Never towed."

"Brilliant, utterly brilliant!"

"Yes, we've refined the parking process to perfection."

Jack put his arm around my shoulder. "Shall we put our faces forward?"

We were surprised to find several couples waiting outside the club, their collars up against the winter wind. The couple in front of us were jogging around in small circles. The girl wore glasses and was overweight. Her down jacket was a mistake. Her date was wearing a very uncool black coat, like my father wears to the office, and had gross skin. I glanced at Jack with pride. I really lucked out, I thought as the guy touched his fingers to his date's cheek. She smiled at him, and it was clear they really had something special going. This was no random Saturday-night date for them. I found myself smiling at them.

"Why are we waiting out here?" Sabrina asked, putting her hand in the pocket of Carl's coat. "I'm going to freeze."

"They have a doorman."

The girl in front of us turned around. "They don't let

everybody in. Friends of ours warned us. You say you're friends of Eddie's or Walter's, and then you get in. They're very choosy."

"La de dah," I said to Jack. "Did you know this was one of these snotty places?"

"All the good ones are these days. Think of it as crowd control. Someone is managing our evening for us. So some boob doesn't throw up on your shoes while we're dancing."

Sabrina looked ill. "What a horrid thought! Jack, where do you come up with such ideas?"

"I've lived longer than you have, my child."

A thuggy man came to the door with a clipboard. He motioned the first couple inside and motioned the second couple away as if they were selling mouth odors. They hurried off, too embarrassed to argue with him. We all moved up in line. I wondered how he decided.

Some kids behind us offered Sabrina a slug of beer from a bottle hidden in a brown bag. "No thanks," she said.

"Come on, lovely. You're the best-looking cookie in line. You're a shoo-in. Mind if we trail along with you?"

"Move off," Carl snapped. "The lady is with me, and we don't need any crashers."

Sabrina stood rigid. I switched places with her. "Hey, they don't mean any harm. They're jerks—pretend they're not there, and they'll go away." She still looked frightened.

"Hey, look at her hair. Hey, honey—" The jerk whistled at me, and Jack turned around, about to get ugly, when the doorman came toward us. "You two guys bug off, or I'll get security to drop you a few miles across the river in Brooklyn. I don't want to see you within blocks of Face Forward again.

Sorry, girls. Why don't you all come with me?" He smiled at Sabrina, then caught sight of the couple in front of us.

"They with you?" he asked Jack.

"Never saw them before," Jack answered gaily. We were getting caught up in the celebrity of the moment. All the people in line were watching us. The doorman glanced at them and jerked his finger over his shoulder. "You folks would be more comfortable someplace else," he said softly.

The guy held up his hand confidently. "Walter sent us."

"Don't know any Walter," he answered wearily. "Why don't you go to Rachett's? They don't have a door policy." He turned to Jack. "They try all the names in the book. The biggest bow-wows always try it. They know the rules—if you don't have the face, you're not settin' foot in the place. It's house policy. Only beautiful people."

"That true?" Sabrina asked Carl.

"I guess so." he looked uncomfortable.

"Well, then, I'm going home." Sabrina grabbed my hand. "You don't want to stay, do you, Jess?" She lowered her voice. "Look at those poor suckers. They were so excited about tonight." The couple who hadn't passed the test were helping each other down the street, arms around each other, as if hurrying from the scene of an accident. "Who needs a place like this? I wonder why they all slink away. I wouldn't. I'd call a solicitor. I'm going to ask Clive—he knows all about posh clubs in London and in New York. I bet they can't keep you out because you have zits!"

Looking at Sabrina, the doorman's manner changed. He became a real toad. "Excuse me, miss, I phrased it wrong. It's not only faces we look for." He laughed rudely. "We got some real witches inside, if that's what you're worried about.

64

But you wouldn't want to spend your evening looking at tacky, offensive types, would you? Of course not. We are protecting our clientele, making certain that you get the quality time you're entitled to." Perspiration was beading his upper lip. "You gentlemen understand?"

Jack slipped him a folded bill. "You are merely doing your job. I was here over Labor Day for Terry Stevens's birthday. That was a dynamite party—"

"Yes. Mr. Stevens took over the club for the night. We permit that only for our very special friends." The doorman put his hand under Jack's elbow as if he were royalty. "How good to have you with us again."

"Please, Sabrina, I'm prepared to blow an entire month's allowance on this place. I wanted you to have a special evening, all of us, a celebration. Come on, honey. You can't help being beautiful."

She appealed to me. I shrugged. "I think it's scummy, too, Sabrina, but as long as we're here—" I was glad Stanwyck wasn't there to witness my cowardice.

Once inside and seated at our table, I had a chance to look around while the waiter took our order. The soft, pinkish lighting made everybody look like TV stars. Small spotlights poked through the dark ceiling, like stars, and lit small vases of roses on each small shiny black table. All very slick. The waiters looked like soap stars; there wasn't a chipped tooth among them.

"Where do warty folks go for a good time these days—into the sewers?" I was playing with Jack's fingers

"Let's drop all this holier-than-thou crap." He snatched his hand away. "We aren't hurting anyone, not depriving anyone of food or clothing or a place to live. So let's have a good time." I thought of Stanwyck fighting across the computer screen with Freddy. At least she couldn't see how angry he was. I was not equipped to fight. Sabrina, seeing how desperate I must have looked, did an about face. "It is a nifty place. Utterly. I'm glad we're here. Let's forget all that nonsense at the curb. Jack's right—it's not as if we own the place and are making the rules."

"Sure. If it were our place we'd let in all the wrong people, the unbeautiful folks." I laughed.

"I wouldn't," Jack said meanly. "We're entitled to our fantasy world, where all the people are perfect—like us."

Of course he was joking.

"Did you read about that kid who got lost in the subway tunnels playing Dungeon and Dragon?" asked Carl as we waited for our drinks. "My dad said the mayor was getting calls from bummed-out parents all week. Can't they close the tunnels, send cops down there, do something to make sure more kids don't get into the maze and get lost?"

"What was he doing down there?"

"Looking for the Dungeon Master. Following clues—some nonsense like that."

"There was a kid in our dorm who flunked out last term because he spent the year playing those games. School was merely a backdrop. All he did was make spaced-out phone calls and leave cryptic notes in the boiler room for other cadets like himself."

"I don't think kids were into that gig in London. What's it all about?" Sabrina was eating a third slice of pizza as if she'd been deprived of food for weeks. I'd never seen her so ravenous.

"One of those scenes like you're caught in a sandpit with

sandworms, here's a map to get out, make your choices carefully," I said, thinking of the notes pinned up on the walls of Noah's bedroom.

"It's heavier than that," said Carl. "Kids get so involved, they believe it's really happening. That's why the kid went into the tunnels to find the wizard. He's been at the game so long, he's forgotten it's fantasy. Under the streets of this city are miles and miles of deserted tunnels, homes for rats and kids who aren't wrapped too tight."

"It's not funny. They must be pretty wigged out to believe all that nonsense." Noah wasn't that squirrelly. He described what he did as *games*—that must mean he didn't believe the fantasy the way the kid who got lost underground must have.

"If you got messages on the phone and in your mailbox a couple times a day about the knights needing your help three levels below the castle, you'd follow the instructions to get to the next clues."

"People don't get so caught up in games," I insisted.

"Ever hang out with guys watching the Superbowl?" asked Sabrina.

"Or girls watching *Dynasty*?" countered Jack.

In spite of its rocky beginning, the night turned out to be a definite twelve on a scale of one to ten. As we were getting ready for bed, the phone rang. Sabrina dove to answer it before it could ring again and wake her parents. She picked it up, listened for an instant, and hung up.

"The breather? A weirdo?"

Her eyes blazed with anger. "What a stupid thing to say!

It was the wrong number! Why would a weirdo be calling me?"

. "They pick numbers at random from the phone book, Sabrina. I didn't mean he was your personal breather. Lighten up!"

"Sorry, Jess. You read so many horrible stories about freaks in New York, I get spaced out when the phone rings late. Please accept my apology. I didn't mean to be rude."

"Don't get so intense." I rolled over and pulled the covers over my head. "Lighten up!"

As I was falling asleep, I thought about what Stanwyck would say about Face Forward. I'd go down to the loft tomorrow as soon as I got up. Cheer her up about old Freddy. Stan'd never go into a place called Face Forward. A shiver went through me. What if the doorman had tried to turn Stanwyck away? Nonsense—she had more style than all the people on that sorry line combined.

"It's double bucky you could come down today. Sorry I've been such a prune. But I've been totally bummed by that fight with Freddy. Once we decided to run the board together, I thought everything would be smooth downloading. Freddy and me forever. Never occurred to me we'd control-s over details. I was too uptight. Who cares if we let crackers on the board? If he still wants to rename the board Saltine— get it, *crackers*?—well, that's all right with me."

Stan often gets attacks of emotional speeding, where one phrase runs into the next. All you can do is dummy up and hang on for the ride.

"Enough chitchat. Let's boot the system and check the postings." Stan twisted her hair around her hand and pinned it up on the top of her head, out of her way. "You're going to be blown away when you see how many new users I've got. I owe everything to Freddy. I've downloaded all my utility programs to him. I did this neat program for timing the amount of log-on time new callers get. First time you call, you get fifteen minutes on the board, the second time twenty minutes, the third time you become a regular. That program took me weeks to get all the bugs out. It kept bumping callers off the board—"

"We went to this ripping wild place last night, Face Forward. You ever hear of it?" I might as well have been talking to the furniture. When Stan gets near the keyboard, she tunes out everything else. "They have a door policy, they keep out the grungy types."

"That's odd, I can't get the files up." She punched a few more keys, then looked up at me, her face a study in horror. "It's crashed! The system has crashed! I've lost all the files on the hard disk! My board is dead!"

"Nonsense, you must have hit the wrong keys. You couldn't have crashed it. Didn't you just turn it on?"

"I edited some postings before I went to bed last night, but I haven't checked it this morning."

"It can't crash when it's off, right?"

"I always leave the board running. I have a responsibility to my clients."

"Then the board was on all night. You mean the computer was on, and the screen was blank?"

"Because it crashed." Stan burst into tears. "I can't get into the operating system. I'm zapped, I'm zero."

Chapter Six

It took Stanwyck forty-eight hours to adjust to this mortal blow. She was a basket case all day Sunday, lying on her bed, bemoaning her fate, then getting up to try different commands to analyze what had happened to her hard disk.

"It's weird, Jess. Something's hanging the system. It's programmed to reset itself. There are utilities built into the operating system that guarantee the system can't freeze this way." She chewed on the end of a pencil. "It's as if someone had dropped some secret control sequence into my operating system." She rolled over and tossed the pencil across the room. "I sound like a character in one of Noah's fantasies. No one could slip a phantom character string into my code."

Since it was Sunday, she couldn't call the hard-disk manufacturer's help line. She did of course call Freddy immediately. He offered suggestions, all of which Stan had tried before she had called him. I think she knows reams more about programming than Freddy. Why else would he have wanted all her BBS programs?

"Well, I guess you'll have to reformat, start from scratch."

"At least you can download all my program files back to me," she said happily.

"I could do that," he answered, "but I don't have the time this week. Maybe next week. I've found this supercooperative dude with a dynamite board who is thrilled to act as a screen for my pirates."

"He's teasing, waiting for me to get desperate," she assured me when she got off the phone. But I wasn't so sure. As far as I could see, Freddy Frobisher couldn't be depended on to help his own mother out of quicksand.

Noah promised to call his programming contacts for ideas. But Stan didn't hold out much hope for Noah's friends. "All those D and D kids are alike. All they want is fresh instructions from the Dungeon Master so they can scuttle through danger-filled tunnels under imaginary castles, killing off knights and paladins who don't exist."

"Maybe one of them will know something real." I wondered why she couldn't download data files from some other sysops and start reprogramming her special BBS refinements, but I was afraid to ask. Stupid questions send Stan up the flagpole on a good day; today they would send her into orbit. When she covered the computer with a quilt, claiming it was dying, I decided to go home.

I wasn't surprised that Stan was not in school on Monday.

"So her computer's on the fritz. That's a reason to stay home from school?" Lulie looked smug. "I don't think Stanwyck's got both oars in the water these days."

Sabrina came to Stan's defense. "She must be very clever to be able to program her machine to time calls, and to keep track of all those passwords, and to let callers read messages on all thirty-four BBS with only one keystroke."

"How do you know so much about it?" Lulie glared at Sabrina as if she'd turned into a toadstool.

"The twins have one of those modem gadgets. We signed on to Stan's board one evening, just to see what it was like. I have a cousin in Milwaukee who calls the Headboard every night long distance. Loves it. Thinks Stan is the best sysop in the country. I have to admit, I was impressed. Although I'm not the best judge, since I'd never seen any other board in operation. She's written little poems and news summaries, like a small-town newspaper. I liked all that stuff better than the phreaker things."

"But to spend your energy on something so boring!" Lulie giggled. "And the boys involved should all be named Nightcrawler or Weasel."

Sabrina shook her head emphatically. "No way, Lulie. Carl said she's got one of the first multiuser boards in this area. That means more than one person can call the board at one time. Calling most BBS, you get busy signals for hours. Stan has a fine system, and she's programmed all these special options. She deserves pots of credit."

I liked Sabrina for being willing to swim upstream for Stanwyck, who usually treated her with thinly disguised scorn.

"Defend her if you want. She was so squirrelly at my party, I was afraid the college crowd would think we were all micronerds at Benchley." Lulie tossed her head theatrically. "Wouldn't it be nice if that rumor got around town!"

"The college crowd?" I giggled. "Come off it, Lulie. It was the twins and Jack—not exactly a crowd. Why don't you cut the digs at Stanwyck? I told you that her computer crashed because I assumed you'd care. It may not be a tragedy to us, but it's devastating to her."

Lulie turned to Meg and Sabrina to see if she had any support. "If I understood half of what she was saying—"

She didn't convince anybody.

Stan wouldn't talk to me on the phone Monday night. Tuesday she wasn't in school. As soon as our English test was finished, I got on the A train and headed for SoHo. When I arrived at the Baums' loft, I entered another world. I should have realized Stanwyck wouldn't take this disaster lying down.

Mrs. Baum was sitting in the kitchen, surrounded by boxes of herbal tea. "I love the antique pictures, don't you, Jess? Look at those delicate leaves. You can almost smell the aroma." She held up a box of camomile tea. "I think I'm going to paper a wall of our bedroom in tea boxes. Won't that be original?"

"Certainly will. Probably get featured in one of those decorating magazines my mom reads. Is Stan okay?"

"I'm in here because they've taken over my living room. They started arriving yesterday afternoon. I had no idea Stanwyck knew so many of these hacker children. Two of them slept on the couch last night. Their dirty feet all over my upholstery. Don't their parents worry when they don't come home? The little one with the dark eyes, Noah? When I insisted he call his father, he said his father works two jobs and wouldn't even know he wasn't at home. That's no way for a child to live."

"I bet the hard disk will be up and running any minute, and you can reclaim your living room."

Mrs. Baum stared disconsolately at her collection of tea boxes. "I have a feeling these kids are never going to leave. I told my husband at breakfast we should cross our fingers her foul computer never gets fixed. But let's not fool ourselves. Stanwyck has never given up on anything she wants. She's the most single-minded human being I know. She'll find an answer to this riddle. Her father has called the experts who installed his system at the factory. Nobody seems able to cure Stanwyck's sick computer. I hope it's over soon. Those boys are not my idea of house guests."

"How come I can't hear them?" I asked, nibbling on a cinnamon cookie.

"They don't talk. They sit at their screens, and every few hours they order out Chinese." She pointed to a couple of shopping bags filled with garbage. "The runoff from this morning."

"Moo goo gai pan for breakfast?"

"It's another world, my dear." Mrs. Baum gathered up some of her tea boxes and went off to her bedroom.

The living room looked like an office at NASA or the Pentagon. Noah sat at one computer; two guys I didn't know were sharing a second computer. Stan and Martin—her friend Captain Midnight—were at her computer, shaking their heads like doctors consulting about a dying patient.

"Hi, Jess. We've tried almost everything, and we're no closer than we were on Sunday. We've run the diagnostics, and there's nothing wrong with the hard disk itself. Hardware and software check out. We keep getting the same message: i/o error. Look at this: 254 bad sectors. It's like saying the entire disk is rotten."

"It's got to be the utilities," Martin said, doodling in ballpoint on his shirt cuff.

Noah frowned. "The hard-disk helpline was the worst. They suggested reformatting the disk, starting all over. What jerks."

Martin looked at me. "You want to see what I've got so far? If we change one line number in the program and reformat the utilities, putting in an end statement—"

"Don't bother, Martin. I'm only good for ordering Chinese. I don't understand the first thing about programming. It's all magic to me."

He and Lulie have the same who-let-you-in-here look.

A boy who looked as if he should be called Rodent licked his lips and hunched over his computer. "We can't do anything with her hard drive, right? No program files, no data files. But the hardware isn't damaged. I tell you, it's someone hanging her system, not something. It's sabotage, and until we find out how they did it, we'll never get the program files back."

"You sure your back door was protected?" one of the guys said, looking up from his screen.

"Mrs. Baum had special locks put on all the doors after Stan and I were held captive in the elevator by robbers," I assured him.

They all burst into laughter, including Stan. She put her arm around me. "The back door is a piece of programming code, Jess. It's the secret way to crack into a program. Once you've hacked the back door, you enter a program and alter the code."

I had no idea what she was talking about. "It's got to be Freddy. He's the only one who knows your programs," I said thoughtfully.

"I told her that yesterday," Noah said triumphantly. "He's the likeliest suspect. He's got the lousiest rep in the country. Most crackers hack for the challenge, to open up a program and see how it's made. They care about computers. He does it to duplicate programs, to sell them. If any one person is responsible for the bad press crackers and hackers have been getting, it's your friend, the great Freddy Frobisher." Noah spoke with more passion than I'd ever seen in him.

Stanwyck jumped up and bore down on Noah as if she were going to swallow him. "You rotten-mouthed little ruggie! You don't know anything except those mindless fantasies. Freddy told me to keep all you rodents off the board. 'Write a program that bumps ruggies soon as they log on,' he said. But I said no."

Noah looked frightened. "I'm sorry, Stanwyck. Don't get angry."

"What is a ruggie?" I whispered to the kid next to me.

"Short for rugrat. A word you use on boards where you can't swear openly. It's the worst putdown, especially of guys like Noah, who do the role games so intense, night and day. Bet he doesn't log in more than two days a week at school. Spends every waking hour logged on to the game. If they've got a computer room with an online connection in his school—forget it. He's in there every study hall, probably cuts half his classes."

I thought about Noah's bedroom, where the sun never shines. What was wrong with the boy's father, letting him live inside his computer?

77

Stan was still standing over him. "Not one more word about Freddy." She snapped her fingers close to his ear. "Or you're going to be posted as a luser on every BBS I know. And that's a promise."

"What's a luser?" I asked the kid who seemed to know everything. He had scrawled scraps of programming code on the sleeves of his Mickey Mouse sweatshirt.

"A user no one wants on his board."

"I have an idea," Martin said to Noah. "You've got the modem over there. Let's access the Pirate's Guide board and ask the sysop if we can download his galaxy files. Start building up your board from scratch."

"No!" cried Stan. "I don't want the word out all over the country that my board has crashed."

Martin laughed sharply. "Why do you think I came over yesterday with my computer? Coincidence? I was in the neighborhood? Come on, Stan, everybody knows. Your friend Frobisher posted everywhere that you were through. It's all over the Pirate network, all the Applers, even the TRS-80 boards. I'll bet by this time even the kiddy-candy boards are posting the news. We'll all do what we can to help, but your board's dead."

Noah was hunched over his keyboard, his face twisted into a frown. His screen was covered with directions about getting three spells from the magic-user before he would be able to advance to the next level. He had only three hours of real time to accomplish this task. He looked up at me, hair clinging damply to his forehead.

"I got up at four this morning. That's when the game comes online. I played until six, caught the bus to school, went to the computer room, played through first period, then went to science and then English, had a study hall and lunch, which gave me another couple hours with the game. I cut my algebra class—hope we didn't have a quiz. Then I caught the train into Manhattan and came over here. I have only three more hours, as you can see. And the game goes down at midnight."

"When do you sleep?"

"From midnight to four. I don't need a lot of sleep."

"And your father doesn't unplug you now and then?"

"He doesn't need much sleep, either."

Stanwyck threw herself onto the couch. "I was one of the best national boards, wasn't I, Martin?"

"You had first-rate modifications. I was proud to say I knew you. But you know elite boards are the hot thing now. Why not reformat and start an elite board—maybe twenty or thirty top-ranked crackers? A blue-chip operation."

"I like being a national board. I want to have the most users. You know how crackers collect ware?" Stan sighed. "Well, I collect users."

"What worries me is, I think we could get caught in a ragwar," the guy in the Mickey Mouse sweatshirt said. He looked at my puzzled expression and grinned. "You never heard of ragwars, right? Well, it's pirates fighting it out. Dropping control sequences into the ware they give out. Then when someone tries to rip off their system—zap! Everything gets scrambled."

Stan sat up, her arms around her knees. "I don't know much about ragwars. I've heard about them, but I've been absorbed in writing sysop programs for the past few months."

"Okay, cracker A gets into a game, let's say Galactron. After he gets rid of the lockup code, he adds his own pirate's title page, like a fingerprint, to prove the crack has been his handiwork."

"A pirate's title page?" Stan looked interested.

"Before he gives out copies of his cracked game, cracker A adds a special sequence. When the game boots, a window opens and his name is drawn through the window, as if pulled by magic forces. That's the cracker title page, and it's usually more fun than the real game title page. If cracker B tries to crack the code for that sequence, there's a piece of code that will glitch the guy's copy of the game. But sometimes cracker B is clever and gets into the code and finds the secret sequence, deletes it, and begins using cracker A's code. Then if cracker A or any of his friends hear of the crack, they'll add a rag page to all the games they crack. It's a page slandering cracker B. It'll appear on every cracked copy of the game, all over the country. In about a week cracker B would be dead meat. Except that cracker B will retaliate. Slip in his own rag page. And zounds! You have a ragwar."

Stan seemed to be in safe hands. With all these hackers lounging around, someone would figure out how to undead her hard disk. I needed to breathe fresh air. The Baums' loft reeked of old gym socks.

"I got to get home. Come on, Noah, walk me to the train."

He gave me a vacant look.

"Earth to Noah. The next clue is underground, near the Spring Street subway station candy counter."

"That's not funny," he muttered. "Candy means a lot to a magic-user. This new game is the cleverest. The way the Wizard Master sets the clues, you have to analyze all the words that seem common. In this game they don't mean what they seem."

Stan was too involved to say good-bye. Mrs. Baum was back sitting in the kitchen arranging tea boxes. "Good-bye, dear Jess. If you come up with any brilliant ideas about how we can reclaim this apartment, do let me know. These awful little boys—oh, hello, dear." She peered at Noah. "Where's your jacket?"

"Didn't wear one." He stared at the ground.

Mrs. Baum sent me a see-what-I-mean look. I put my arm across Noah's shoulders. "Come on, kid. Let's blow this fruit stand."

In the bright afternoon sun, Noah looked out of place. His pasty skin and slicked-down hair were in sharp contrast to the hearty people coming out of the art galleries along West Broadway. Poor Noah seemed like an alien from one of his fantasies.

"Want to come to my house for dinner?"

"Can't."

"You could call your dad from a booth and ask."

"Can't. I have too much work."

We crossed the street and paused at the stairs leading down to his subway to Astoria. "You and Stan live at the opposite ends of the RX train. What a lucky coincidence."

"Everybody lives somewhere." His chin sank into his chest, as if he were protecting himself from a great wind.

"I don't live close to any subways. I'm a bus person."

"I've been taking the train since I was too young to pay the fare. I know all the trains like the Wizard Master knows spells."

The ground shook as a train rattled through the station

below our feet. "Hope you didn't miss your train, standing here talking," I said.

"Makes no difference. I like waiting in the station. I shut my eyes and see if I can open them at the exact moment the train's headlight shines through the tunnel. I wait at the head of the platform. I always sit in the front car. It's like running the train."

"Is something wrong? You seem so sad, Noah."

"She won't believe me." His eyes were shiny. "Freddy has a terrible rep. Everybody knows he's a real dude. A cowboy who can't stand to be crossed. He's the one who got into her driver. I don't know how he did it; he is the cleverest dude. But she's never going to get her system up and running again, and if she does, he can knock her out whenever he wants."

"Noah, nobody has that kind of power."

"He's a paladin. He's progressed to the highest level. He's going to win the game."

"It's not a game."

He looked at me briefly. "Everything's a game."

Chapter Seven

When I got home from school a couple of days later, Jack was sitting in the living room with my mother. His long legs were stretched out in front of him. His arm was stretched across the back of the couch. For the hundredth time I marveled at his calm manner in Mom's presence. For most people my mother is not an easy person to hang out with. She asks questions that have no answers, like "What are we going to do about those dreadful horns honking?" "Why do people get stuck in traffic driving across the bridge?" Usually my friends feel obliged to offer some sort of answer. Not Jack.

"How was Stanwyck, dear? Did she come to school? Her mother's been so depressed with those people mucking up her house."

"Stan came to school, but the hackers are still at the loft. They don't go to school on a regular basis."

"It's been about a week since she blew her system?" asked Jack.

"I have never agreed with the Baums' permissiveness. Remember, Jess, I don't expect a repeat of that police business."

I grinned. "Don't worry, Mom. This is a desperate situation. But not with cops and robbers. This trouble is all contained inside the computer and in the programs. Getting it fixed calls for desperate measures. Stan's whole system is locked up. All the programs she's worked on for the past few months for her bulletin board? They've disappeared electronically. They simply don't exist."

"Why is that such a disaster?" Jack asked, taking a sip of his beer.

"It wouldn't be for Jess," Mom said proudly. "Or that lovely Sabrina. Stanwyck is high strung. She takes these things too seriously."

"Mother!" I tossed my coat on her white chair. She flinched as if I'd hit her with it. She'd never say anything nasty, not in front of Jack, so she got up, took the coat, and disappeared into the back hall, offended.

"She is pretty involved in that BBS—you've said so yourself."

"Haven't you ever been involved with something that took over your life for a while?" I asked. I hadn't forgotten Jack's callousness the night we went to the pretty people's club.

He reached for my hand. "Not with a machine." He flashed me a glistening smile. I sat next to him, stretching my legs out alongside his. No doubt about it. He was poster material.

"The sad part is, I think her friend Freddy is the mole."

"Doesn't he live in the Midwest somewhere?"

"I don't claim to understand it. But he sounded almost pleased when she told him the dilemma on the phone."

"Could we talk about our date tonight, just for a minute?"

"We had a date?"

"You thought I was taking your mother to dinner?"

As if summoned to answer the question, Mother appeared in the doorway. "Telephone for you, Jess. Sounds like long distance."

"I'd take another beer on your way back," Jack said.

"Hello, dollface. Bet you don't know who this is," said the voice on the phone.

It was a male voice, smug, full of silent laughter. "Tell me who you are this instant or I'm going to hang up," I said.

"Don't do that, honey. It's Freddy, Freddy Frobisher. Isn't it just too terrible what's happened to your friend Stanwyck Baum, operator of the greatest BBS in the country?"

"I thought she was your friend, too."

"Nobody's board is better than mine, doll. For three years I've had the hottest boards anywhere. She tried to one-up me. Luckily, I'm the forgiving type. I'll retrieve those files. But I need a little encouragement, pretty lady. And that's where you come in."

"Freddy, did you crash Stan's system?"

"You have such a low opinion of me. I'm very hurt."

"Get on with it, Freddy. I'm on my way out for dinner."

"I can't convince your friend Sabrina to go out with me."

"Sabrina!"

"Most beautiful girl I've ever seen. When I was at your school, she was wearing a green sweater. I dream about that sweater. I'm willing to fly to New York, take her anywhere she wants to go, a hot evening on the town, and she won't even talk to me. Imagine that!"

"What does your striking out with Sabrina have to do with Stan?"

"If I came to New York to go out with Sabrina, I could stop by and reprogram Stan's system. Probably take all of twenty minutes, and she'd be so happy, our little BBS queen."

"If Sabrina won't go out with you—"

"Pay attention, Jess. I'm going to call Sabrina in three hours. If she says yes, then Stan's board will be up and running by tomorrow evening. Otherwise she can start from scratch, and it'll take her a month to rewrite all her BBS programs. See you on the boards, honey."

I stood next to the telephone shaking with anger. If Freddy was the only one who could fix the system, Stanwyck faced a silent keyboard and a blank screen.

"What's up," Jack asked. "You look like you want to strangle a grizzly."

"Freddy Frobisher," I said.

"Who's he? My competition?"

"Could we go to Sabrina's before dinner? I'll explain everything on the way."

Sabrina's parents were out for the evening. The apartment smelled of burned food and oregano. Sabrina led us into the kitchen, where the twins were rolling out dough for a homemade pizza. Tomato sauce dribbled down the front of the stove, and the table was covered with grated cheese.

"Just in time for Dr. Carl's magical pizza, cure-all for the insatiable appetite."

"We're not hungry." I sat at the table and picked up the

cheese grater. Jack ate a handful of olives and began rummaging in the refrigerator. "There's a problem, and Jack thinks I should be open and tell you all what it is." I explained about Freddy's call.

Sabrina turned pale. "He must be the one who's been calling," she whispered.

"Those calls! Your squirrelly look when you came back to the dinner table the other night. Freddy Frobisher!" I cried. "The snake."

"It's been a nightmare." She wept. I rummaged in my bag for a tissue. Carl put his arm around her and led her to a chair.

"For the past few weeks I've been getting these calls from a guy. He tells me he thinks about me all the time, carries on about my silvery silken hair in an eerie way. Wouldn't even tell me his name. As soon as I pick up the phone, he starts talking. Always the same business. He asks me to go out with him, says he knows all the fanciest restaurants in New York, tells me how much money he has. Calls me dollface. I hang up, and he calls back a few minutes later, like the night you were here, Jess. He says I'll change my mind, and then he starts laughing at me. It's been awful."

"You never told me." Carl sounded indignant.

"I never told anybody. My folks are nervous about my zipping around town alone. They're not strict, really. You see, we heard such stories in London about crime in New York. A wacko calling me is the excuse they'd need to pack me off to boarding school in England. I figured as long as he kept calling, he couldn't be too angry with me, so he wouldn't do anything weird."

"You took a humongous risk." Mark shook his head.

87

"Somebody's got to teach this scuzzball a lesson," said Jack.

The twins nodded in unison.

Sabrina's eyes were filled with tears. "You understand why I can't go out with him, Jess? I'm sorry about Stanwyck's machine. But I can't."

"You think I'd want you to?" I said, incredulous.

Mark began spreading tomato sauce on the dough. "What about calling Ian, the grok down the hall in our dorm who's always in the computer room? He could figure out any sabotage this Freddy creep could invent."

"Excellent," said Carl. "We can saddle up the horses and ride hard all night to rescue the hackers. Mount up, cavalry! It's time to get our computers in a circle!"

"What about the pizza?" Mark licked some sauce from his fingers.

"Is that how the West was won?"

Little had changed at the loft. It was like entering a time warp. Martin had the hard-disk manufacturer's system manual open and was reading off strings of code to Stanwyck. Two of the hackers, hunched over another computer, didn't acknowledge us when we roared in the door. I did feel like the cavalry, dragging Jack's ex-roommate Ian across the huge living room to meet Stanwyck. She was acting the role of a lady in distress. All that was lacking was the applause of the people in the theater and the popcorn.

"What are you all doing here?" Stan asked.

"We've brought Ian to fix your computer."

"I don't need your help. We've got everything under control."

I pulled Stan into the bathroom and closed the door. "Have you lost your mind? This guy is one of the computer wizards of Columbia. Jack says—"

"I don't give a fig what Jack says. I don't need the beautiful people to bail me out. Now, take Miss London and the college crowd, and control-z."

"Sit down, Stanwyck," I said through clenched teeth. "And don't say a word." Surprised at my tone, she obeyed.

"Your Freddy has been hitting on Sabrina."

"That's a lie."

"The creep's been calling her on the phone, trying to get her to go out with him. He called me a few hours ago to say he'd fix your computer when he comes to New York to go out with Sabrina. No Sabrina, no BBS."

"I don't believe a word of it." Stan pushed out her lower lip and twisted one of the candy-colored guest towels folded on the edge of the sink. "I'm not going to lose him to her," she whispered.

"It's a real bummer, but the guy is a megacreep. You're not losing him. Sabrina won't go near him. He's been using you."

"No!" She swiped at her tears with one of the bright pink towels. "You don't know anything about Freddy. You've been so tied up with Jack-be-nimble and his crew. Freddy calls me every night. He's so funny. You've never looked through the printouts of some of our conversations. We built the BBS together. He said I was the smartest girl he ever knew."

"You are smart, but you're much more than smart. You're funny and kind and my best friend." I tried to put my arm around her, but she huddled into a corner, holding the towel to her face as if she had a toothache. "None of that changes because Freddy is a twerp."

She closed her eyes. "They all know what a jerk I was."

"They're here to help you. They know he was using you, but that makes everyone loathe Freddy. Believe me, they're not laughing at you. You've got to give people a chance instead of assuming they're out to put you down."

She glared at her reflection in the mirror. "Have I looked this gawky all day?"

I laughed. "All week."

"So all our hopes are riding on this grok friend of Jack's? Actually, he's kind of cute in a microchip sort of way." She winked at me and rebraided her hair.

Ian picked up the systems manual, impatient to begin. "You downloaded all your program files to this other person? Well, clearly he got into your back door, changed the codes for one of the utilities. Which means your files still exist."

Stan grabbed his arm. "They do? I don't have to start all over?"

"All we have to do is unlock the piece of code he dropped into your operating system, which is bypassing—"

"You think you can fix it?" she whispered.

"Did you have any password or routine to boot the system, any batch files?" Ian sat at the computer with the other hackers around him. Sabrina and I went into the kitchen, where Jack and the twins were eating cold Chinese food from cardboard containers. "How revolting," I said, It occurred to me that with all the munching Jack had done in the past two hours, this was dinner. I picked up a fork and poked through some stiff pieces of pork and clumps of damp rice.

90

"It's time to plan some revenge on Freddy," Jack said.

"Let's get the system running first," I pleaded.

"I don't care a fig about the board, Jess," said Mark. "It makes me sick to think of Sabrina being hit on by this creep."

"We could call the FBI," said Carl. "He's been in trouble with them before. Maybe they'd lock him away for a few decades."

"For calling me on the phone?" Sabrina giggled. "I'm not a national treasure or a military secret."

There was a knock at the door.

"Couldn't be the feds already," said Mark, pretending amazement.

I opened the door. A slight man dressed in a shabby overcoat smiled hesitantly. "Are you Stanwyck Baum?"

"No, I'm Jess Graham."

"Let me introduce myself. Abraham Kurtz. Is my son Noah here?"

"I haven't seen him. Would you like to come in? I'll check with Stan."

I took him into the living room and tried to get Stanwyck away from the computer. Mr. Kurtz waited nearby, his eyes wide, the way people react at the Haunted House at Disney World. He ran his fingers over the driftwood coffee table, speaking to no one.

"Maybe I could help you. Stan is kind of busy," I said, leading him back to the kitchen. He didn't have the decisiveness of most adults.

"My son isn't here?"

"No one's seen him in a couple of days."

"I found this address on his desk next to his computer.

91

With these directions." He pulled a piece of paper from his coat pocket. On one side was Stanwyck's address and phone number. On the other were some numbers crossed out and a few phrases that had to be directions: "Go down the steps, thirty-five, thirty-six, go past the magic outlay, RX. Two paladins. The silver is in the shop where the cleric blesses the bones. Use short bow. Where is the sword?"

"I don't understand this message, Mr. Kurtz."

"It's difficult to admit," he said in his dry tone, "but I do not know where is my son, and when was the last time I saw him."

Sabrina gave a warning glance at the twins, who were imitating the man behind his back, wringing their hands the same way he was. "Could I fix you a cup of tea, sir?" She pointed to the stacks of tea boxes on the counter. "It's a specialty of the house."

"That would be kind. I work at night, recreating the works of Gemaliel, an early Hebrew rabbi, from the fragments of Babylonian parchments found near Schechem." He looked up at us. "You are not Jewish," he said flatly. "But my son, he does not have interest in these things, either. Only computers. His mother died last year, and she used to help me with my work. Now I must work twice as hard, because I work alone."

"Do you remember talking with Noah? Having breakfast with him? Walking to the train with him, perhaps?" Sabrina seemed to be taking charge. Jack threw me a let's-get-out-of-here look. I turned my attention back to Mr. Kurtz. His pale hands had the dusty look of parchment.

"It was not yesterday because I slept in the library. It was maybe the night before, but you see, he spends his nights playing those games over that modem device, so if I try to call him, I get only a busy signal. Last night there was no busy signal." His voice shook. "There was no answer at all. So I thought he was asleep. When I got home today, he was not there, and the mail was in the box. Noah always takes in the mail."

Mark and Jack were studying the paper. "I think these are some of those dungeon game clues," said Mark. "Perhaps they're directions from his Wizard Master. Do you have any idea which game he's playing?"

"Are there different ones?" Mr. Kurtz smiled shyly. "It is confusing to me. I spend my days in the first century, you see. With the rabbis before the destruction of the Temple in the year seventy, and my Noah is in the twenty-first century with creatures from other galaxies. I always say there are two thousand years standing between us. Not a good way for a father and son to know each other."

"Ian will know which game the kid is playing." Carl brought his friend into the kitchen. Ian's face was flushed. "I think we have the answer. We'll be able to restore the files momentarily. You see, Freddy bypassed the directory, so no matter how you boot the system, the batch file can't sequence." He examined the paper Mr. Kurtz handed him. "It could be almost anything. Not enough clues for me to tell who his Wizard Master is. But the business about the cleric blessing the bones sounds like a new Pit game that's being played on an elite board called Funhouse. We could try to contact the sysop and see if he knows where the game is at this point. Maybe talk to the Wizard Master. See what clues and directions he's given Noah the last couple days."

Stan stood in the doorway tugging at her braid. "He plays Funhouse. For sure. I think he's living out the game to the max. For that group of ruggies, it's the ultimate challenge."

"What do you mean?"

"I was so wrapped up in the board crash, and I was mad at Noah for blaming Freddy without any proof! I didn't pay attention. He'd never been a magic-user before. He was having trouble with the new role. For the first time, the kid was stumped. Couldn't work out the pattern. He got imprisoned in a catacomb and didn't have the equipment to get out. This is all my fault. He's imagining dungeons under the streets. The subway tunnels must be the catacombs. He's underground. He's forgotten it's a game."

"Like Alice falling down the rabbit hole." Sabrina handed a cup of tea to Mr. Kurtz. "Don't worry, we're excellent game players. You wait here. We'll bring him back within the hour."

"A magic-user! Like the priests from those mystery cults in early Palestine." He seemed to be as caught up in his own fantasies as Noah was. No wonder they didn't have dinner together. They couldn't agree on a century.

"We'll call you in half an hour. Perhaps you could nap." Sabrina set the teapot on the table next to Mr. Kurtz. Amazing person, that Sabrina. She had me almost convinced we could find Noah. As if New York were the size of a computer keyboard!

"Now, you call the sysop, Martin, and see what you can find out about this Wizard Master. We need to know what the last clues were to each player in Noah's group, especially his last instructions to Noah."

"What's the kid's handle?" Martin asked.

94

"Mr. Rogers."

Predictably, everyone in the room groaned.

We left Mr. Kurtz stirring sugar into his tea. Stanwyck had more color in her face than she had in weeks. "Just like old times, Jess. We'll find him. I think we should split up. Each couple can take one nearby subway station. Ask the token taker if they've seen Noah. Meet back here in an hour. Jess, come with me." Stanwyck took my arm.

It was cold, and the wind was blowing bits of litter across the street. Jack put his hand on my other arm. "Jess is coming with me."

"It doesn't matter." I felt embarrassed at the way he and Stanwyck were glaring at each other. "Jack, you and Stan and I can go to the E train. Sabrina and the twins to the A, and you two"—I pointed to the nameless hackers standing together—"can try the B train."

"Those trains don't go near Astoria. What about the RX train?" shouted Mark.

"That's the train! We were walking home from the loft a couple days ago. He was very sad. I said he and Stan lived on opposite sides of the RX. He said something about tunnels. What if he thought the RX tunnels held the clues he needed to escape from the catacombs?"

"There are miles and miles of them. We'd take days tracking him through all those dank disgusting tunnels," moaned Carl.

"I read there are alligators in the tunnels." Sabrina shivered.

"No one's ever seen one. Besides, I'll protect you," Mark put his arm around her. His twin immediately put his arm around her, too. Poor Sabrina was almost crushed between them.

95

While we were running through our plan one more time, Ian came running down the block. "We've got it restored! It *was* the directory, Stanwyck. You are back in business!"

"Now we put Freddy Frobisher out of business," Mark snapped.

"I don't want revenge," insisted Stanwyck. "Is there a way, Ian, to knock him off the board if he tries to get into my program? So he can't wreck the board again?"

"We'll put a mole in the program. I'll go back to the loft and start working on it. An extra command before the entry password to crash his utility files. He'll never know it's sitting in his binary drive."

"I want revenge," said Mark, his face dark with anger, "for what he's been doing to Sabrina. Who's with me?"

Stan shook her head. "It's my decision. This is not about Sabrina."

"Could we decide this after we find Noah?" I asked. "Freddy will keep. Noah may be in trouble."

The Spring Street subway station that was assigned to Jack and Stanwyck and me was one of the scrungiest in the city. The old tiled walls were cracked and coated with grime. There were two men collapsed next to puddles of rain in the stairway. A couple of empty whiskey bottles were discarded nearby. "Bet they haven't seen Noah," whispered Stanwyck.

The air smelled of wet clothes and dirty bathrooms. It was inconceivable that Noah was roaming around down here for fun.

"Count the steps going down," suggested Jack. "Maybe those numbers refer to steps."

There were eighteen steps down to the first level and another twenty-two down to the next level. There was neither candy nor a newsstand, and no other people were in the station.

"Let's go the edge of the platform and shout his name into the tunnel," I proposed. "Well, we can't squeeze *into* the tunnels. When a train comes, we'll be squashed like bugs."

Jack and Stan both laughed. "Lucky for you, I used to hang out in the tunnels," said Jack. "When I was in high school, we had a fraternity initiation in the tunnels under the BMT. Had to walk from the Eighty-sixth Street station to the Seventy-seventh Street stop. There are little platforms you stand on, built into the sides of the tunnels to protect you when the trains come whistling through."

"Forget it. We'll contact the police if we don't find him. They can search the tunnels." I shook Stan's shoulder. "I mean it."

We shouted Noah's name, but the tunnels were so vast that our voices, even shouting together, didn't carry very far. After ten minutes we gave up and went back to the meeting place. The others hadn't met anyone who remembered Noah.

"We'd better call the police." Sabrina sighed. "Poor Mr. Kurtz."

"We'd better not call the police. You know how they feel about phreaking. We'd better solve this ourselves."

"No way, Stanwyck," I said firmly.

"There are tunnel maps in the city planner's office. At least I think there are. I remember rolled-up maps, don't you, Carl, last summer when we worked for Dad? I know for sure there were detailed maps for the water department, because I had to catalog those."

"Clever brother! We'll lift the key from Dad's ring. Then

97

we can pretend to be doing work in the Municipal Building. It's a piece of cake. We've borrowed city equipment for a lot less, I assure you." Mark grinned at Sabrina. "We'll find him."

"Who's going to tell that poor little man?" Her voice quivered. "Noah is all he has in the world, except for those fragments of parchment he studies."

"He's probably asleep."

"Or dreaming about some lost century."

"The kid is as good as home."

Chapter Eight

Sitting in the backseat of the "official" city car, waiting for the twins and Sabrina to return with the keys to Mr. Nelson's office, I had time to think. Noah could have been missing anywhere from a few hours to three days. It was hard to imagine living with a father who could dim out for three days at a time.

Martin and his hacking buddies had been hanging out at Stanwyck's loft for a week, and the phone hadn't exactly been ringing off the hook with concerned parents. I wondered if kids with parents like mine—bloodhounds who track your every move—could get as involved with their machines as the phreakers. Even Stan's parents would ground her for a week if she didn't come home for a couple days. And according to Mom, Mrs. Baum's rating as a parent is a bit lower than that of the old woman in a shoe.

Jack isn't comfortable with the hackers. He depends on people's responses to him. When we're together, he's constantly looking at me to see how I'm reacting to whatever he's said. To have an expressionless computer screen staring at him like a lidless eye twelve hours a day would be true punishment. It made his vow to return to the loft and begin composing a rag page against Freddy all the more touching. Surrounded by these hackers who give him the creeps, he was trying to get Stanwyck out of this terrible hole, even though she was clearly not his favorite person.

I leaned across the seat and opened the door. Mark went around to the driver's side. It was eleven o'clock. The streets leading to the Municipal Building were deserted. Ten minutes later we were parking the car, running through the scam. "Why can't I be more excited about this?" I whispered to Sabrina.

"Because that poor boy may be in trouble."

Her beautiful face was clouded with worry. She's a lot kinder than I am, I thought, stifling a yawn. I didn't hold out much hope for finding Noah. I couldn't imagine how he could believe beasts were chasing him through the tunnels, much less that medieval paladins could require him to produce a spell to remain undead. Even for a game phreaker, this was stretching credibility. After studying the maps of the tunnels, the others would recapture their common sense. By morning we'd dump the whole thing into the lap of the police.

"So old Jack is writing a wicked rag page." Carl laughed. "When he's through, Freddy Frobisher will wish he'd never heard of Benchley phreakers."

"On the phone he sounded utterly determined he'd have

his way," said Sabrina, shaking her head. "Anyway, a rag page has to go on a piece of software that phreakers are crazy to collect. We don't have software to tempt them."

Mark tapped out a rhythm on the horn. "That's what old Ian is doing even as we speak. He's cracking that new Zounds! game that Stan's dad bought to cheer her up. It hasn't been released yet. Mr. Baum got it from a friend in the business."

"Mr. Baum gets everything from friends in the business." I laughed. "That man knows somebody in every business you can think of. From pedometers to the script for next week's *Miami Vice*."

"A good man to know," remarked Carl. "Now, let's get to it. You girls give us about ten minutes, then come in and talk to the guards. Say you're waiting for us. Make it all seem legitimate."

"That's not smart," Sabrina said. "If anyone ever checks up on people going into that office tonight, they'll remember a great crowd of us. Now, the clever thing is for Jess and me to stay out of sight. If you were truly working, you wouldn't have brought along dates. Get serious!"

"Whatever happened to sweet Sabrina from England?" Carl tickled her under the chin.

Sabrina was not in a mood for games. "Carl, you stay outside, too. Mark, go in alone."

"Why him?" said Carl. "I'm twice as clever as he is."

"Actually, we may have to search a number of desks and files to find this map. I'll need him if it isn't going to take all night."

"Well, don't call attention to yourselves," warned Sabrina.

"People always remember identical twins," Carl told her.

"You know, Mark, that map was in the long cabinet behind Mr. Jowles' desk. I remember seeing it last summer when I was recataloging the water and sewer pipe diagrams."

"Jess and I will wait in that little coffee shop across the street. I hate waiting in cars in the dark. Too much like the opening scene of a horror film." Sabrina opened her purse. "Do you have money for coffee, Jess? I have only loose change."

An hour later the boys joined us in the coffee shop. Three cups of tea were sloshing around in my stomach. I had called Mom to say I was staying at Sabrina's. She had told her parents she was staying at my house. Everything was set for our long night in the subways. My mouth stretched into a huge yawn. "We'd better get moving, or I'll fall asleep in my teacup like the dormouse in *Alice in Wonderland*."

Mark cleared away our cups and spoons. Carl spread the map across the table. It was one of those architectural blueprint maps more than two feet across. There were twenty pages of diagrams. "There's an entire city underneath the city!" I leaned close to the diagram, trying to read the tiny print. There were numbers in boxes every few inches along the squiggly tunnel lines. We had no idea what the numbers signified.

"Doesn't matter what the numbers mean."

"Unless they're the number of people trapped in the tunnel since the last map was drawn," joked Mark.

Sabrina gave him her coldest look. "Finding Noah is what this is all about. Cut the jokes."

"You don't even know the little twerp," said Carl. "Why are you acting like a general moving your troops into battle?"

Sabrina smoothed her hair off her face. "I had a younger

brother, Teddy. He was drowned at a summer picnic four years ago."

I felt cramps in my stomach. Stanwyck's nasty comments about Sabrina and her overprotective parents ran through my mind. She'd be devastated to learn what the real reason was that Sabrina called home when she was on a date.

Mark kissed her cheek. "We'll find Noah."

"Look here," Mark cried. "I think this is Houston Street, and this is the RX train going up to Spring Street. Give me that red pencil. We'll follow it along. Now, here it goes, look at the length of this tunnel. Here's a side tunnel. There are no tracks here. Wonder what it's for?"

"There are several branching tunnels without tracks. Can't tell from this diagram if they end at a stone wall or whether the mapmaker stopped drawing since it wasn't a part of maintenance track."

"I think we're on to something," I said. "Walled-up tunnels would be close to dungeons, wouldn't they?"

Sabrina nodded. "How are we ever going to check out all these tunnels? There must be fifty miles of them."

"We're going to need huge flashlights," I reminded them, "especially if they're dead-end tunnels."

"Let's stop at that all-night camping goods store near Fourteenth Street and then drive back to the loft." Mark was writing up a list of supplies. "We'll need whistles to signal each other. Maybe a couple of walkie-talkies. So we don't get lost."

Some adventure, I thought, yawning behind the over-stuffed shopping bag on my lap. "So far computers have brought nothing but trouble to my life," I complained. "And don't any of you dare lecture me about the benefits of hightech."

Mr. Kurtz was sitting at the table exactly as we had left him, a spoon in his half-drunk glass of tea. "You did not find Noah," he said.

"We did find a map that will lead us to him, sir."

"There's an entrance to the lower level of the tunnels right near here. At the Spring Street stop. We think that's a clue because Noah mentioned spring to Jess."

"That's right. It meant nothing at the time. He said his Wizard Master needed powders before spring."

"This is dangerous?" the old man asked.

"Not at all," Carl assured him.

I wished I were as certain as Carl. Walking along those narrow parapets to get to the branching tunnels was going to be hairy.

Sabrina sat across from Mr. Kurtz and looked at him intently. "Do you remember anything Noah might have said about this new game he was playing? If you let your mind wander, don't think about the games or the clues, just think about the last few conversations you had, maybe something will come to you." She went to the stove and turned on the flame under the kettle. "Some hot tea might help."

He sighed. "How fortunate to have found such young people. Noah has better friends than he has a father."

Not knowing what to say, we left him staring miserably into his tea.

Jack and Ian had taken over the computer in Stanwyck's room. No one was permitted in there. Martin was scanning the boards, looking for clues about the new game, which was apparently called Dark Spell. Stan was on the phone with the Funhouse sysop. "Listen to me, Paul Bauer. I'm not some dippy ruggie looking for clues. I'm a sysop, same as you. If you don't give me the Wizard Master's number and this kid is never found, you'll be in jail for real. No electronic dungeons, but the concrete slammer!" She screwed up her face and hunched over the telephone, cradling the receiver between her ear and her shoulder. "It's not a threat, it's an observation. Based on verifiable evidence."

"Tell him Captain Midnight will download him a copy of Zounds! Newest cracked ware. He can be the first board to post it," Martin suggested. He turned to me with a wide grin. "And do us a favor at the same time. He can begin getting out the rag page to the elite crackers. What a day for phreakers everywhere! Getting rid of Freddy Frobisher!"

"Don't write him off yet. He's probably got a hundred schemes up his sleeve. Scuzzball like that doesn't quit."

"It's time to move out," Mark said, rolling up the map. "We've got to get into the tunnels while the trains are on the slow night runs. Lucky it's the weekend and we don't have to cope with rush-hour commuter crowds."

Stan handed a slip of paper to Martin. "Here's the clown's number—Paul refuses to give us his full name. In case I get the urge to call the feds. Apparently there are only about ten kids playing Dark Spell. It's very exotic. Paladins and magic—there're no knights, no gunpowder or dynamite. It's supposed to be more of a head trip. And that's all Paul knows. Or that's all he's admitted knowing."

"You coming to the tunnels, Stan?" I zipped up my jacket and clipped a flashlight to my belt loop.

"Of course." She tossed back her braid. "Finding Noah

will be the first story we get out on my new board. 'Sysop hero rescues ruggie.' "

Sabrina seemed reluctant to leave Mr. Kurtz until Martin promised to try to get him to take a nap. Sabrina put a blanket on the living-room couch and allowed herself to be dragged off by Mark and Carl.

The cold night air reminded me that this was not a game, not the amber abstractions of the computer screen. Real subway tunnels. Real kid missing.

The subway station was deserted. Even the two drunks were gone. "Let's go to the head of the platform. He told me he likes to pretend he's driving the train." At the edge of the platform dozens of crumpled candy wrappers were stuck to the billboard. If you squinted they spelled out *undead*.

Stanwyck leaped into the air. "Score."

As we approached the edge of the platform, my heart was pounding. I had always been afraid of falling off the platform. Without hesitation Mark jumped onto the tracks. He turned and held up his hand to Sabrina. "No big deal. Jump." She closed her eyes and jumped, and Stanwyck followed. Carl looked at me. "You nervous?"

"Terrified. They look very small down there. It must be farther than it looks."

"Just the perspective makes it appear that way. C'mon, I'll jump with you. It's not a long drop."

"Don't think about it, Jess. Jump!" Stan shouted. "We don't want to be standing here when the train comes roaring through."

"Yeah. Honk, honk, peanut butter!"

"Not funny, Carl."

I shone my flashlight down to the cinder bed below. I

could see crumpled newspapers and candy wrappers on the tracks.

"Pretend it's a hot summer afternoon and you're jumping into a cool river in Maine," Mark suggested.

"Stop badgering her." Sabrina looked up at me. "You could wait for us right there. We should have someone who can run for help in case something happens."

I grabbed Carl's hand and stepped off the platform. My knees were trembling as I landed. I fell against Mark, knocking him to the ground. Sabrina helped me up, and we began walking down the deserted track, wondering when we'd see the menacing headlights of a train. "Where is the ladder to the platform?" Stan asked, her voice echoing through the tunnel.

"Should be another couple hundred yards, no more." Mark shone the beam of the light onto the far wall. No sign of a ladder.

"Are we certain there's a ladder?" I asked. The cold damp air hurt my nose and felt raw in my throat. I doubted Noah would have leaped off the platform into this sooty darkness, but those candy wrappers stuck to the billboard were a sign.

Mark trotted down the track, scanning the walls with his flashlight. Chalked to the wall was a message: BRENG CLEAR THE CATACOMBS.

"It's the Pit game!" shouted Stan. "We guessed right."

Carl took my hand. "Can't be more than five minutes to the next station. There's got to be some access route to the deck."

"Over here, a scaffold," Mark shouted.

"Be careful. We don't know how sturdy it is."

"It could be rusted out at the back. Don't put your weight

on it," called Stan, running to where Mark had begun to shake the scaffold to test its strength. I ran after her and stepped into a puddle, splashing filthy water on myself and on Sabrina, who had been running alongside me.

"This is the pits," she muttered.

I could hear Noah in his ratty little bedroom telling me, "Most of those who venture into the pit never return."

"Think how awful it would be down here alone. I'm losing my nerve, and there are five of us." Sabrina shivered. "Smell's like the inside of my dad's fishing boots. Old rubber."

As Mark began to climb the scaffold, Sabrina made soft noises in her throat. I saw in the shadows that she had shut her eyes tight against the sight of Mark swinging out over the tracks. "He's not going to fall," I whispered.

She opened her eyes and gasped. "Carl! Look! Way down the tunnel."

A round spot of light—the headlight of a train.

"Quick—climb the scaffold." Stan and Carl hung on to the scaffold. I couldn't move. Sabrina dragged me to the side of the track. "Come on, Jess!" she cried. The tunnel was brightly lit now from the headlight of the oncoming train. I stared at the light, transfixed.

Carl must have grabbed me. I felt myself being lifted into the air, his arms tight around my waist. "Hold on to that crossbar, Jess!"

Stan reached over and clutched one of my arms. Mark yanked at my other arm. "My legs won't hold me!" I cried. "I can't find the step!"

"You're on the step, you're safe—just hold on," Mark told me.

"Don't look down."

"Don't look at the train."

Sabrina climbed up another couple of rungs.

The tunnel was filled with piercing light. I squeezed my eyes shut. The scaffold shook as the train rattled past us. My hair blew into my face. After the train disappeared down the tunnel, I still heard it squeal and grind.

We were silent, holding on to the cold metal scaffold. Finally Mark spoke, his voice hoarse and a bit wobbly. "We've probably got another twenty minutes before the next one. Shine the light on the wall, Carl, and I'll check out the area behind the scaffolding." He slipped between two of the widest metal bars and climbed down the other side of the scaffold. "Guess what, fellow cat burglars!"

"I'll bet it's bad news," Stan said.

"The side tunnel is covered with a metal grill. They must be doing some reconstruction that doesn't show on our map."

"We never checked out the date of the map." Carl groaned, clicking the light off and on in frustration.

"We'll have to use the maintenance deck to get to the Canal Street Station. The next side tunnel is below that station, if I remember correctly."

"How long before the next train?" I asked, hoping someone would suggest we go home. "We might be spotted by the conductor, and then we'd be in deep."

"Doubtful, Jess. When the train came through, the engineer wasn't looking for people clinging like monkeys to the workman's scaffold," Stan said reasonably. I marveled at her calm. "Passengers were probably sleeping. They aren't going to see us because they aren't looking for us."

Mark hauled himself onto the catwalk and surveyed the

tunnel. "It's a piece of cake walking up here, and it's not as sticky."

"How far are we going to walk on this deck?" I grumbled, hiding my sweaty face from my friends. They all seemed nimble. When it was my turn, I grabbed Carl's outstretched hand and to my relief discovered climbing onto the deck was a lot easier than climbing the scaffold. Once we were on the platform, it felt much wider than it looked from below. Cramps gnawed at my legs. I fought against the dizzying sensation that I was going to fall onto the tracks.

"Hey, Noah!" shouted Stan. "Are you down here?"

"Calling Mr. Rogers," I said in a softer tone. The echo carried my words down the tunnel. About a hundred yards ahead we could see the red and green lights of the next station. A welcome sight.

"As I remember the maps, the next side tunnel is about fifty yards past the next station." Mark said. "Wish we had some nuts or candy. Suddenly I'm starved."

I thought of Mr. Kurtz idly stirring sugar into his glass of tea, trusting that we'd find Noah.

"It'll take us a week to work our way down the RX all the way to Queens," remarked Carl, as though reporting an interesting fact.

"We can't explore during the day. There are track maintenance crews scheduled all along this line," Sabrina said. She shone the beam of her flashlight along the wall. "See these piles of tools? We'd be caught for sure."

"There's no sign of any kid here," Stan said, her shoulders slumped in defeat. "What made us think he'd be in the tunnels?"

"He came down here when we left your house the other

day. And the paper did say RX," I said. "I wish I didn't think he was down here. But we should check out the side tunnels— they've got to be his dungeons."

We'd come to the end of the maintenance walk. There was a ladder built into the wall. Mark climbed down a few rungs and leaped a few feet onto the station platform. My throat closed in panic. I'd rather get caught on the narrow catwalk than take the chance of falling onto the tracks. Carl picked up a shovel that was lying nearby. "Here, Mark, grab the end of the shovel. Jess, climb down right behind me and put your feet onto my shoulders. I'll hold your legs to steady you. Reach out your right arm and grab hold of the other end of the shovel—"

"I can't."

"Sabrina, you go first," Carl said. "That's right. Put your foot on my shoulder. Don't be gentle, darlin', put your weight all the way down. Squarely on my shoulder, like it was a rung of the ladder. You're not heavy. Now the other foot. Grab hold of the shovel. Now I'm going to lean toward Mark, and you're going to step onto the platform. It's only a step away. Balance yourself with the shovel. Good girl."

"Ready now, Jess."

Stan crouched next to the ladder. "I'll steady you from this side. You feel a lot shakier inside than you actually are. Pretend we're in gym class."

"Don't think about the tracks. It's rock solid ground under your feet you're stepping across."

It was their strength of will that got me onto the platform.

"You want to go home?" Mark asked as the light of a train lit up the station.

111

"I'm sure slowing you guys down," I said, my face red with embarrassment.

"That's not what he meant." Sabrina shook her fist at the train. "I'll never be able to ride the train again without remembering how it felt on that scaffold." She put her arm around me. "I was as scared as you, Jess."

Of course! I didn't have the copyright on terror. Immediately I felt tougher. Strength flowed into my legs. "As long as we're all shaking, let's get into that side tunnel."

"It will be easier this time," Mark promised.

Surprisingly, he was right. I got down the ladder on the first try.

"We have fifteen minutes till the next train," I reminded them.

"Mark! Jess! Carl! Can you guys hear me?"

"Did you hear that?" Sabrina clutched my arm.

I looked up to see Jack and Ian leaning over the platform. "Are you weirdos down here?"

"Lord, supposed they've been bug-juiced by a train." Ian's flat nasal voice echoed through the empty station.

"We're here, you turkeys." Mark waved his flashlight around the area of the tracks where we were standing. "We've searched every inch of the tunnel from Spring Street, and there was no sign of him, although he left us a clue."

Jack waved a sheet of paper. "We have the last clues that mugwump wizard gave the kid. He said the kid called him voice for the clues. Said his computer was down. There was a lot of noise on the phone line. Had to repeat the clue several times before the kid got it straight."

Ian lay down on the platform and leaned his head and shoulders over the edge to talk to us. "I think you've been on the wrong track, ha ha. The last clue is 'Look for the Dean of Dentyne. Find him before you get chewed out.' "

"What in blazes does that mean?" Mark shivered.

"Could it be gum, chewing gum?" asked Sabrina.

"It's very damp down here. I sure could use some hot coffee."

"Let's go back to street level and rethink the plan," suggested Stan. "My fingers are stiff with cold." Climbing back onto the platform was much easier with Jack and Ian's strong arms for support. I was overjoyed to see the sharp neon lights of Canal Street, where the peddlers were trying to sell everything from fresh fish to umbrellas even long after midnight.

"See that phone booth?" Mark pointed to a booth on the corner. "The kid could have called the Wizard Master there and changed his direction."

Once we were settled in an all-night coffee shop and my hands were wrapped around a mug of steaming coffee, the fear of the tunnel began to retreat. The voices of my friends replaced the sound of the screeching train in my head. We all trembled from the bone-rattling echoes in the tunnel.

Stan put her arm around Sabrina's shoulders. "I think it is chewing gum. Sabrina's right. But what chewing gum has to do with the RX train—"

"One of those kiosks that sells gum?"

"They all sell gum, but most of them are closed at night."

"Except at the big stations like Grand Central and Penn."

"A candy stand would be too obvious. It's not a wizard kind of clue."

"We were at the right station," Stan insisted. "That was a

113

clue—'undead candy bars.' Noah's playing against us now, not the Wizard Master."

"The guy on the phone wouldn't tell you what he meant?" Carl asked Jack.

"He said he had no idea how Noah would have interpreted it. He's never been to New York and has no hidden agenda about the subway tunnels in the game. He said that gum was one of the items used for trade in the Middle Ages. Noah could use chickle, like spices, to trade for some of the powders he needs for spells. The guy thought I was weird. He felt it was necessary to remind me there were no subways in the Middle Ages!"

"There was no Dentyne gum, either," Stan complained.

"That's it!" I shouted. "Remember, Stan, when we were kids, the Dentyne factory, somewhere in Queens?"

"I do remember a gum factory. It had giant sticks of gum on the outside of the building."

"I remember that place, too," said Jack. "But it was Black Jack. I thought the gum was named for me."

"You would," muttered Stan, catching my eye.

"It's too late to go to Queens tonight," I said.

"Nonsense, we've got the official car," said Sabrina.

"We could check out the gum factory and be back at the loft before dawn," said Mark, counting out money to pay for our coffees.

"That is the best news!" I felt a burst of new energy. Dentyne was gum. I didn't need to hack out fantasy games to know that. It was the most solid clue we'd had.

Ian had been trying to get Stanwyck's attention. "And I've cracked Zounds! Haven't had this much fun since we brought down the American Express overseas operation a couple summers ago. During the tourist season." He opened his mouth in a soundless laugh. "You may want to put the finishing touches on the rag page yourself, Stanwyck. When we get back, I'd like to run your utility programs. You've got a beautiful programming touch—a total zinger."

Stanwyck, deep in conversation with Sabrina, seemed not to have heard him. "Down there in the tunnels, especially when we were hanging from the scaffold, you had nerves of steel. I forgot you were beautiful. You were just a friend."

I looked up in alarm, but Sabrina was smiling.

Chapter Nine

"This is no circus clown car. No way all of us are going to fit," said Mark matter-of-factly. I wondered if everyone else was as ready to give up their place in the car as I was. Of course I was concerned about Noah, but my shoulders ached and my eyes were gritty from lack of sleep.

"I'll go back to the loft and run through the Zounds! program code one more time. To make sure Frobisher is ragged once and for all." Ian grinned. "I don't know Noah, wouldn't recognize the little ruggie even if I fell over him. What about you come with me, Stanwyck, so we can check out the rag page? I bet you've got some insults I never even thought of."

"Good idea," she said eagerly. They set off down the block. Sabrina pulled me aside. "Would you mind terribly if I went back to the loft? I'd like to see to Mr. Kurtz. I remember how the waiting was for Mummy. And she had Daddy and me and Aunt Posey."

"Of course I don't mind. I'll keep the twins from stepping on each other's toes. And Jack will come with us. We'll be back in an hour or so."

"Wait for me! I'm coming with you!" Stanwyck was running down the block, her braid swinging from side to side. Puzzled, Ian was standing where she'd left him, arms crossed, shaking his head. It would take him longer to get used to Stan's quirks than the few hours he'd needed to break the Zounds! code. "Sorry, Jess, I got carried away. Mention program codes, and I'll follow you anywhere. But Noah is my responsibility. The poor kid probably wouldn't have taken off like he did if I hadn't been so involved in perfecting my codes that I treated him like an epsilon."

Sabrina gave her a quick hug. "You're beautiful, Baum," she said. They both grinned as if they shared a humongous secret.

Mark couldn't resist the opportunity of going back to the loft with Sabrina. So Carl and Jack and Stanwyck and I got into the car and drove over the Queensborough Bridge, looking for the old factory with the sticks of gum on the outside.

Carl headed east on the parkway, following the signs to the airport. "Do any of you have the slightest idea where the place might be?"

"We used to see it on the way to my cousin Harriet's. They lived in a white house about an hour from our apartment on Fiftieth Street."

"Good, Stanwyck. That puts us right at the door of the factory."

"Okay, Black Jack, got any better clues?"

He put his arm around me and hugged me close. "You haven't said a word."

"Let's stop and ask directions."

"Sensible Jess." Stanwyck sighed. "A wizard master for real."

Carl pulled into the next gas station. "Could you tell us how to get to the chewing-gum factory that has the sticks of gum on the outside?" But the guy walked away, assuming we were jerks out to bug him.

We tried an all-night doughnut shop, two guys waiting for a bus, and the people in the car next to us at a traffic light. Nobody knew about the factory. We drove around aimlessly for another fifteen minutes. Queens seemed pretty boring except for one funny building with acid-green spotlights shining all around it. "Looks like the palace of Oz," remarked Stanwyck as we drove past.

I almost fell asleep against the warmth of Jack's chest. "This is pointless," I murmured.

"It could be worse," he whispered into my ear.

We could be hanging from that dreadful scaffold, I thought, burrowing my head into the folds of his sweater.

Carl honked his horn and signaled to a police car that had pulled up next to us. They laughed when he asked about the factory. "That place burned up about three years ago. Arson. It was a falling-down wreck. Half the windows were broke. Haven't made gum there for a decade. I think it had been used as some kind of warehouse."

"You can't make gum in the middle of the city anymore. You make it in Taiwan, where labor is cheap," the other cop said.

"We need to know where it was." Jack leaned forward to get closer to the window. "We are supposed to meet somebody there. Kind of a scavenger hunt." He flashed his dazzling grin.

"Not far. Take this road about three more lights, go around the traffic circle, and follow the detour around the new waterfront construction. You'll come to a fenced-in area—it's a sewage treatment facility. One of the buildings in that complex used to be the gum factory."

First subway tunnels, now sewage. I had reached my limit. "This is crazy. He's not going to be at a sewage plant. How would he have got there? Hired a limo?"

"Jess is right. It's a dead end." Carl pulled over onto the shoulder of the road. "I say we drive past the plant just so we can tell Mr. Kurtz we tried everything we could think of, and then we call the cops and report the boy missing, which is what we should have done in the first place."

Jack agreed. "We only assumed he was following that loony Wizard Master."

"Please give me half an hour to check out the area," said Stanwyck. "You all wait in the car. I have to know for myself that he's not there. He grew up in Queens, he'd remember the gum factory. Noah is a very determined person. I've watched him unravel clues of these role-playing games. He never gives up, and we can't give up on him. Please!"

No one said any more until Carl parked the car in front of a twenty-foot high chain-link fence. He turned to Stanwyck and waited, expecting the padlocked entrance to the fence to settle the issue. "I'm no James Bond," she said as she got out of the car, "but then again, neither is Noah."

"She's megaweird, your friend," said Carl, turning off the engine.

"What else is new?" Jack didn't sound irritated. Carl went across the street to buy some coffee, and Jack and I snuggled down in the backseat. To be honest, I didn't care if Stanwyck took an hour sleuthing.

"Why can't she admit defeat?"

"Stanwyck has never lost at anything. She's like a dog looking for a bone she buried last summer. It never occurs to her that she's not going to find it."

"You saying Freddy Frobisher wasn't a bone she wanted?"

"He was hardly her fault. That creep." I sat up and straightened my hair. "I should go help Stanwyck."

"Did I say the wrong thing?"

I climbed over into the front seat. "Isn't there a subway map in the glove compartment? My brain must have been on hold. Where is the end of the RX line? I've got to find it on the map. We have to follow the route to the nearest RX station. That's the connection we overlooked."

A fine mist of rain had begun to fall. If frogs and toads began falling out of the sky, it wouldn't surprise me this night. "Stan, where are you? I've got the map." I ran down the street with Jack and Carl following close behind. "Can't we at least take the car? It's raining," grumbled Carl. "There's got to be a better way." He wiped his face on his sleeve. The rain began to fall harder. "You're as loony as she is."

Stan pointed to a bus shelter. "We can study the map under there." She unfolded the map, which we tried to shield from the rain with our jackets. "Quick, before it melts." Jack laughed.

"I circled the whole fenced-in area calling his name. Not a

121

creature was stirring," Stan said. "Glad you guys are here."
She smiled weakly. "I feel as though this is all my fault."

"The RX line is marked in green," Carl said gruffly. "Now,
here's the highway and that traffic circle we passed, remember?"

I huddled against the back of the bus shelter, wishing I
had worn a heavier jacket. On the overhang were the neatly
printed words DEAN OF DENTYNE. STUDY NOTHING IN BETWEEN.

"Look! He's been here. He's telling us it *is* the gum
factory."

Stan shook her head. " 'Study nothing in between,' " she
repeated. "He means the opposite, Jess. It's not the sewage
plant. 'Study Dentyne' means something else. He must have
thought like we did, that it was the gum factory but realized
it could never be the sewage plant. We're close to it, close to
him. Time to move on."

"To where?"

"Let's get in the car and ride the RX line from Noah's
house back to Manhattan," Jack said, looking at me for
approval.

"I wish it weren't true, but we'll do better on foot," I said
as rain soaked into my collar and drizzled down my neck.
"We're only about four blocks from the Forty-fifth Street
station. Let's go."

"What would he be doing?" wondered Carl. "Read me the
clue again."

" 'Look for the Dean of Dentyne. Find him before you get
chewed out.' "

Jack clasped my hand, and we headed into the rain.
"Dentyne, Dentyne, Dean of Dentyne," chanted Jack, swinging our arms as we walked along.

Aside from the occasional car speeding past, we were the only people in sight. I suspected that we were all equally discouraged, but it was easier to walk around in the rain than to go back to the loft and face Mr. Kurtz with the truth.

"Wait! I heard it just as Noah must have heard it." Stan shook her head and started to laugh. "Listen! Den teen. What is a den of teens?"

"A den of teens would be a burger joint, or a school."

"That's it! 'Study nothing in between.' Let's look for a school."

"Not any old school." Stanwyck was flushed with excitement. "It's got to be between the sewage plant and the RX line."

"There's probably two or three. It's a densely populated neighborhood."

"There's only one school named for its dean, or principal," said Stanwyck in triumph. "Noah has lived here all his life. It might even be his elementary school."

Three block later we came to Harry Harkins Middle School, a large brick building across the street from the Fifty-second Street RX stop. We'd passed it twice in the car, never imagining it was a major clue. We'd laughed at the lime-colored spotlights that gave it a Wizard of Oz–colored yard, never thinking "den teen."

We ran across the yard, screaming Noah's name. Stan ran up the steps and banged on the door of the school. Carl and Jack began poking around in the bushes, shining their flashlights into the dense undergrowth. Nothing but pop bottles and a red sneaker. Stan and I went around to the back of the school, where there were no green spotlights. The rain had stopped, but a soupy fog was blotting out the light from the streetlamps. I shone my flashlight around the deserted playground. "I'm going to check out that small shed at the far side of the monkey bars," I called to Stanwyck.

My heart was pounding as I ran across the playground. "Noah!"

The door to the shed opened. "We won! We solved Dark Spell. I knew you'd find me!" Noah shouted. Shivering in his gray coat, his face pale and ghostly in the beams of our flashlights, Noah had no trace of fear on his face.

"Noah! You've been missing for two days!" Stan yelled, rushing up to us. "Your father is paralyzed with fear! I'm going to cure you of playing these stupid games." Stanwyck grabbed him and shook him violently. "There are no wizards, no dark spells."

"Have you lost your mind?" Jack pulled Stanwyck off the frightened boy, who hunched over, his body shaking with sobs.

"Why are you so angry, Stanwyck?" Noah cried. "I knew you'd come. I knew you'd figure out the clues. I had faith in you, Stanwyck."

Stanwyck was crying as hard as Noah.

He tried to put his arm around her. "Besides, there was a game cheat. I had unlimited spells. Not just the measly five the Wizard Master gave me."

Noah's father did not shout at his son. In fact, he didn't utter a single word. He covered his face with his hands and prayed, whispering barely audible words, his body rocking gently back and forth. He didn't seem affected by the chaos in the loft.

From the minute we'd burst through the door, the scene

at the loft had been anything but calm. Mrs. Baum carried on enough for parents everywhere. With her hands gripping her throat, she glared at each of us in turn and finally said in a hoarse tone, "I almost died tonight."

"Ma, you never even left the loft," Stanwyck said, trying the reasonable approach.

"I almost died of fright."

"Game, set, and match," muttered Jack.

Mr. Baum, wearing a plaid cotton bathrobe, hovered near the door to the bedroom. "Could we get some sleep now that this thing seems to be wrapped up?" he asked uncertainly.

Mrs. Baum sighed. "If you can sleep when your daughter was almost crushed by a subway train, by all means."

Mr. Baum straightened his back like a soldier preparing for inspection. "Stanwyck, this computer business has gone too far."

"Sir, it's my fault, not Stanwyck's," said Noah.

Mrs. Baum glanced at Noah, then moved toward him. She held her palm to his forehead, took his pulse, and straightened his T-shirt. "How long were you out of touch?" she asked softly.

"A couple of days," he whispered.

"I think it was longer than that." She put her arm around his shoulders and hugged him close. "I am going to see that this child has a bath, something to eat, and a long sleep. Stanwyck, when I come back from the guest room, I want this loft deserted. Understand?"

As soon as Mrs. Baum and Noah were out of earshot, Mr. Baum turned to Ian, who was reading a mass of computer printouts. "Think you can improve on it?" he asked.

"We could write a much tighter program. Each of your

125

sales invoices could be automatically generated as it keeps track of the inventory. Your salesmen would punch only three or four key combinations. And we link up each showroom with each other and with the factory."

"Come over to my office in the morning." Mr. Baum glanced at his watch. "It is morning. Why don't you all get cleaned up, and I'll take everyone to Sanderson's all-night diner for breakfast? There's nothing in this place to eat except cold moo goo gai pan." He glanced at Mr. Kurtz and laid a hand gently on the man's shoulder.

"You don't need me, sir," Ian said. "You've got an ace programmer much closer to home. Stan writes awesome code." Ian looked at Stanwyck, and his face turned red. "Maybe we could write a program for your dad's plant together."

"Excellent," she said. "You've got another Baum on the payroll, Dad."

"I'm going to get dressed." Mr. Baum looked pleased. "You heard my wife. She means business, so you'd all better get your gear together. It's going to seem strange to come home to an empty loft." He paused in the doorway. "Nice strange. Don't feel sorry for me."

Martin pointed to Mr. Kurtz, who continued to pray, oblivious to us.

Sabrina looked around at each of us. "Leave him be. He's had a great shock. This is his way of dealing with it. We all have to keep an eye on Noah. He needs people around him."

Carl nodded. "We could introduce him to the groks in the computer room at school. Kids like Noah have fierce competition to toad for guys like Ian. He'll think he's died and gone to heaven."

Sabrina punched his arm. "Sh. Use some sense."

"You'll appreciate me when you hear what we did to Frobisher's operating system."

The phone rang. Stanwyck ran to answer it before her mother heard it. She listened for a minute, then put her hand over the receiver. "It's Freddy." Her voice had the same hoarse tremor as her mother's.

Surprisingly, Jack looked delighted. "I was hoping he'd call. Tell him we're downloading the new Zounds! to all the major boards this morning. Assure him your board is up and running."

Mark hugged Sabrina. "Tell him to phone up your board whenever the spirit moves him."

"I can't hear," whispered Stanwyck, waving her arms impatiently.

"Suggest that he give Sabrina a ring. Or Jess."

"Have you lost your mind?" I cried.

"Trust me." Jack was the picture of smug.

"I found it with the help of some friends," Stan was saying. "Right next to the binary driver. Yes, you were immensely clever, Freddy. I'd never have found it alone." Poor Stanwyck, I thought. There was still admiration for Freddy in her voice.

"Tell him to call your board and try another maneuver." Jack could barely control himself. He motioned us all to the other side of the enormous living room, away from Mr. Kurtz and Stanwyck. "We got into his program and added a piece of code. If he tries to dial the Headboard number, Sabrina's number, or Jess's, the program will substitute and automatically dial the FBI snitch hotline and dump his files into their database. He'll never know what hit him."

I ran to the phone and grabbed it from Stanwyck. "I'll be waiting for your call, Freddy."

"Who is this?" He sounded suspicious.

"It's Jess Graham. Remember me, the missing link to Sabrina?"

"The looker. Sure, I remember. Why the change of heart?"

"Let's say I realize how much a call from you would mean to my reputation at Benchley. If you call me, I'll be a real hero to my friends."

"Depend on it, dollface. We'll make history."

"Headlines, Freddy. I know we'll make headlines."